THE POWER

Sherian McCoy

WWW.MARTINSISTERSPUBLISHING.COM

Published by

SkyVine Books, a division of Martin Sisters Publishing, LLC

www.martinsisterspublishing.com

ISBN: 978-1-1937273-08-8

Science Fiction/Fantasy

Printed in the United States of America
Martin Sisters Publishing, LLC

SKY VINE
BOOKS

Science Fiction/Fantasy

DEDICATION

To my daughters, Ivy and Sarah, the inspiration behind
The Power.

CHAPTER ONE

Frank flew the helicopter to Cape Cod. He searched for the ground team in the clearing and landed the helicopter in an open field nearby. His footsteps moved quickly on the ground, closing the space with urgency. He watched, with anticipation as the agents put on gear – preparing to invade the warehouse.

He quickly found Agent Lacy Powell and pushed through the crowd in her direction, flashing his badge to the officers – this was routine. Frank had enough adventures to last a lifetime – which is why he craved simplicity, but adventure – dangerous adventure – always found him.

It was unavoidable, he thought to himself. In the wake of all the destruction that seemed to surround Frank's job, he had made a promise to his wife to make things better. Before she died, she wanted to know that he would do his part to clean up the community and protect the environment – it was their dream together. Tonight, this was Frank keeping his promise.

"Do we have movement from inside?" Frank asked Agent Powell. "What's happening?"

He grabbed a pair of binoculars and peered through the glass. He could see the men inside moving back and forth, packing boxes onto a truck inside.

"I didn't know you would be in the field on this one, Frank. I thought you were on undercover assignment in Mexico," Agent Powell said. "A shipment was just delivered. We are going in now to make arrests and find out where the stolen weapons came from."

"I was in Mexico – we wrapped up early and you know this case is important to me," Frank spoke as he put on a bullet-proof vest. "I wanted to be a part of the cleanup. We've worked together a long time – you knew I wouldn't miss this, if there were any way possible."

"I guess I did know that. You're here now, how do you want this to go?" Agent Powell asked, looking around but trying to stay down low, out of sight of possible onlookers. The only light was coming from inside the warehouse through the small open windows. The team of twenty-five agents, dressed in head-to-toe black department-issued gear, kneeled on the ground waiting for instruction.

"I'll take the lead on this one, if you don't mind," Frank said. "We'll go in soft, guys – save the heavy artillery, but watch out. On my command, go!"

Agent Powell nodded in agreement to support Frank's decision. "Follow Frank's lead – do what he says."

She moved aside as the men loaded up on weapons, stun guns and communication radios and moved into position.

"We need these guys for questioning afterwards – it's by the book," Agent Powell spoke into the radio.

Frank waved his hand for the team to move out. They positioned themselves at the entry doors, listening for the signal to go in. Frank could hear muffled voices from inside the building. Then he heard the truck's engine start.

"Move, Move, Move!"

All agents rushed the building, dodging bullets and shooting with expert precision. The criminals toppled over to the floor, from the force of the laser guns. It was going smoothly, but one of them got away and ran toward the back of the building. "Stop – F.B.I.!" Frank chased after him, yelling.

Frank, extremely fit, managed to maintain a daily workout that even Jack called, "rigorous."

Frank leaped over tables and boxes until the suspect was cornered with nowhere to run.

"You're under arrest," Frank said, facing him. But the suspect lunged toward Frank with his fist tightly in a ball. Frank aimed and shot, hitting the man squarely in the chest.

The room was filled with high-pitched screams as the man fell.

"You're going to be fine," Frank told the suspect. "It's not a bullet, but it hurts like hell, doesn't it? See – there's, no blood. You'll live. *And* you're under arrest."

Frank handcuffed the man and walked him outside.

"Where did you get the weapons?" Frank asked.

"I don't know anything about weapons," the man said, keeping his head down as he walked.

"Let me guess. You just happened to be in the neighborhood?" Frank led the man to Agent Powell.

Agent Powell directed her men to take the suspects into custody and read them their rights for further questioning.

"Did he say anything?" she asked Frank.

Frank exhaled, clearly exhausted, "No, he's not talking. Let's see if he feels better after sitting in a jail cell."

"Frank, we're going to find out who's behind the illegal weapons trade. Did you get a lead on the buyers?"

"I think so. I'm going in undercover in the morning to see if I can get a name – I'll let you know how it goes."

Frank turned and waved goodbye.

"Sweep the place nice and clean. Load up the weapons. We don't want these in the wrong hands. Let's move!" Agent Powell spoke authoritatively into the radio.

Frank boarded the helicopter and flew home.

THE POWER

CHAPTER TWO

Virginia Beach was Jack's home. Up until five years ago, he and his dad traveled a lot with his job. But five years ago, Jack's mom made Frank promise to stop moving around so much – so they built a home as close to the ocean as they could. The Atlantic Ocean was his back yard. Even though he was in college now, this was still home. Jack sat alone on the terrace underneath the night sky, cradling his guitar as he played. He sang aloud, as if trying to drown out an unwanted noise. Jack sang louder and louder, leaning over the guitar in a way that made his back look disfigured and awkward. He closed his eyes tightly and allowed the music to fill the air – until there was nothing else.

In that moment … in that space, Jack was free. There was no expectation or judgment; there was no critique of his fashion sense, no one counting the number of girls he'd dated. His dad's words echoed in his ears, "Life doesn't stop just because you're not ready to move forward, Jack – it's not going to slow down and wait for you to catch up – you may as well learn that lesson now."

Frank had a way of saying things like that; his words were like a cold shower – eye opening.

Jack had friends tell him that he needed to "find himself … that's all," they'd say, as if that was the over-the-counter prescription for his ailment. He wondered how he'd even go about doing something like that.

What would the road to self-discovery look like? He asked himself. Jack played until his fingers started to cramp and decided he needed a change of scenery.

He scrolled through his texts from girls whose faces he could no longer remember. The names meant little to him – they were just names on the screen. Jack had closed himself off from most of his friends, except for Adam, who he'd met the first day of college.

They got along like brothers – it was the easiest relationship he'd probably ever had. Jack looked at the clock – it seemed as good a time as any to get out. If he timed it just right, he could catch Adam between study sessions.

Jack took the keys from the table, grabbed his jacket and ran out the door. He tested the limits of his Bugatti Veyron as he sped down the road to Adam's house. He didn't bother to call – after four years of friendship, Jack could usually pin-point Adam's whereabouts with precision. Adam had an identifiable pattern, school, library and the weekly chess club meetings.

Adam had two things going for him: he was good with computers and very good at playing chess. He was actually quite popular for a know-it-all, chess playing, computer geek. Adam was like that, which is why they had been friends.

"Hey, Jack, come in," Adam yelled over the music.

Jack looked around Adam's home. It was actually his family's vacation home and they often popped in during the summer, which drove Adam crazy. It was a very nice three-story waterfront estate. Adam had the place overflowing with different chess games, set up around the room and Jack wasn't allowed to touch them. Adam was obsessive over chess.

"You were a no–show in class today," Adam announced.

Jack ignored Adam's tone.

"I came to see if you wanted to do something tonight, go out where there are actual girls."

"Wow, I'm glad that you chose *me* to be your wing man, but you know that I have a chess tournament coming up, I can't go. I have to focus and be ready for any possible maneuver."

Jack picked up a chess piece, "Yeah, you're a beast dude."

Adam was used to Jack's comments, so he overlooked the cynicism.

"The last time I went out with you I woke up two days later and I still don't remember what happened. No."

"We had fun, trust me," Jack laughed openly.

"My parents wanted to pull me out of school and fly me back to Canada. They were this close to doing an intervention. No way – not gonna happen."

Jack laughed. "I'm sorry about that. This will be different."

Adam showed no hint of caving. "I can't. Anyway, I have class tomorrow and you do, too. Why don't we throw a party Saturday night after finals at your place?"

"Why my place?" Jack asked.

One, you have the pool house. Two, your place is bigger than mine. And three, I don't have to clean up," Adam said.

Jack was never one to turn down the chance to party, but he hesitated at the thought of playing host all night. It was one thing to go out and be entertained by strangers but he didn't want to have to polite conversation and be involved – he knew it was selfish and mixed up.

"I don't know."

"Come on, Jack. I'm starting to worry about you," Adam said. Are we on for Saturday night after finals at your place? Adam took Jack's silence as permission. "I'll get the word out."

Jack sighed, surrendering. "Yes, if it's a small party, Adam. Small! Jack reiterated as he walked out the door.

See you in class in the morning! Adam yelled, as Jack left with only a wave.

Even though Jack was a couple of years older than Adam, Jack thought Adam took on the character of the big brother, always trying to look out for Jack. They had been friends since enrolling in the university and Jack used to be outgoing, even reckless but lately he had become withdrawn and moody. Maybe he had reason to be, initially, but Adam had decided to push Jack back into socialization for his own good.

THE POWER

CHAPTER THREE

It was Friday morning and Frank Prince sat in his office working; tinkering with some gadgets he designed. Frank was a software engineer, who had become well known for his robotics designs and his study on energy. Frank's company had teamed up with the Environmental Protection Agency to use his design as a new fuel source and also to create a battery for a new line of hybrid cars. A battery that never needs recharging not only had the EPA's attention, but Congress was lined up to get a look at Frank's research. Most of Frank's designs were sold to toy manufacturers. It was a nice change from his consulting work with the government, which had lately left a bad taste in his mouth.

Frank took the remote and pointed it at the dog in the corner. Jack named Haley and she was now thought to be a pet, rather than an engineering design. No one would ever guess she was not a real dog. Frank pushed the buttons and Haley's eyes flashed which allowed Frank to see into all the rooms of the house. Frank could see Jack was still in bed, late again for class. Frank sent Haley to Jack's room.

"Go wake Jack, Haley," Frank said.

Jack had changed after his mother died, maybe they both did. Frank was working all the time and Jack lost interest in everything. Both Frank and Jack did a good job of avoiding. Neither of them could admit it but they were waiting for something to change.

Frank welcomed Adam at the front door as usual. He was hoping that Adam would be a good influence on Jack.

"Good morning Adam. Jack's in his room. Maybe you can get him out of the house this morning."

"I will see what I can do, Frank."

Adam noticed the dart board game in its usual place. Adam and Frank had an ongoing challenge on who was the best. Currently, Frank was winning, but Adam never gave up on trying to score better than Frank. Adam picked up a dart and aimed – barely missing the center.

"I'm ready for a rematch – I've been practicing," Adam said.

Frank laughed and reached in his drawer and pulled out an even bigger dart gun. He aimed at the dart board and six darts flew at an impossible speed from the gun, leaving a trail of smoke in the air.

"Any time, Adam – I made this dart gun just for you," Frank said.

Adam's mouth gaped open.

"I can't wait … I think. Um, I'll go check on Jack."

Adam put the dart gun down and slowly backed out of the room. Frank was always one step ahead of Adam and the thought made him laugh aloud from enjoyment. Adam thought Frank was a good father. It didn't hurt that he had neat gadgets around the house and that he was a black ops, FBI agent. That was pretty cool at any age, even though Adam didn't know a whole lot about the spy stuff – it was cool. Jack didn't think his dad was as exciting – maybe he was too stubborn to appreciate him.

Adam entered Jack's room with his usual secret knock.

"Jack, your dad let me in. I stopped by on the off chance you were going to class this morning. You *could* make an appearance sometime — it wouldn't hurt."

Jack sighed. "I'll catch up in plenty of time for finals. I will read the material the day before and — well, I always get an A. It'll be fine. You worry too much."

Adam mocked Jack's attitude and wondered why he bothered enrolling in classes he never attended.

"We can't all have a photographic memory; *I* actually have to go to class."

Adam wasn't jealous of Adam – he actually admired him – that Jack could find something to busy himself, even if it was just to make his dad happy. But Adam knew Jack had not yet found the one thing to motivate him to move forward. It was like Jack gave up after his mother died – and he hadn't yet recovered. Adam tried his best to keep Jack preoccupied.

Haley appeared out of nowhere and lunged for Adam's ankle. Adam quickly raised his feet off the chair.

"Hey, I think your robotic dog hates me," Adam said, looking down at Haley, who was barking at him.

"Yeah, well, she just doesn't think your jokes are funny." Jack patted his thigh twice, "Come here, girl."

Haley calmly moved away from Adam and sat at Jack's feet. Jack had programmed several commands to control Haley – but she was so lifelike that it was easy to forget she was a computer chip inside all that fur.

Adam relaxed. "You need to get out more. Anyway, I told your dad that I would try to get you to go to class –"

Jack picked up his guitar and started strumming. He wasn't really ignoring Adam, but he just wasn't interested in listening to Adam talk about classes.

"I'm pacing myself. I don't want to overdo it," Jack replied.

"You spend more time on the guitar than you do outside the house these days," Adam said, laughing.

"Chicks dig the guitar, man," Jack said.

"Yeah, and how many 'chicks' have you been out with lately?" Adam asked, trying to bring Jack to reality.

Jack had to think about that one – he usually hung out with Adam and he really couldn't remember a recent one-on-one date, unless he counted the time he crashed Adam's chess club meeting and spent all night talking to Sasha and Natalie Anton, twins from Russia, who showed him how to checkmate in four moves.

"Well...," Jack raised the question again.

Adam quickly jumped in.

"Exactly – you can't remember! I've made my point. You're twenty–three. You're rich. You live in a mansion and have more cars than you can drive. You have the hair thing going on. *And* you

15

look almost as good as me – you should not sit at home all day, with only your guitar and Haley to keep you company."

"Correct me if I'm wrong, but, Adam – *you* play chess! *You* are president of the chess club – hardly the chick magnet," Jack said, mocking Adam.

"I play very manly chess, which takes a lot of brute strength and manpower to manipulate my opponents and crush them, leaving them wounded as I go in for the kill – ending with the crescendo check mate…and ….and… well, now, you've made me late – I have to go. I'll call you." Adam turned and ran out the door and down the stairs in a gust of wind, with a quick wave as he passed by the study door on his way out.

*

"Frank Prince, speaking," Frank answered the phone in his office. "Ah, yes, I am Jack's father. I see. I will make sure he gets the message. Thank you." He sighed as he replaced the phone with deliberate exasperation.

Frank marched into his son's room. "Jack, I've just received a phone call from your professor…"

"What's for breakfast?" Jack asked, yawning.

"Lunch is for breakfast," Frank answered. "It's after eleven. Didn't you have a class this morning? How can you manage to miss the one class you're enrolled in this semester?"

"I was just there, Dad. Anyway, who's counting?"

"The professor is counting. That's why I'm here – your professor left this message … "Yeah, yeah … threatening to drop me from the class if I don't show up today," Jack said, glancing at the note.

"Jack, your mother would be so disappointed if she were alive. You're unfocused. You don't go to class. You rarely leave the house. Son, do something with your life."

"Like you!" Jack fired back angrily.

"The least you can do is show up," Frank's voice was tempered. "You know this school work stuff in your sleep. You're talented, you can do anything, be anything, but you have to show up."

Frank turned to walk out of the room, but stopped short. "By the way, I will be home late … I have a meeting."

A disinterested Jack strummed his guitar and waved goodbye. Jack crossed the room and saw Frank driving away in his Maybach. The car didn't seem so extravagant in their Virginia Beach neighborhood. Jack's mom had fallen in love with the property and designed the house, which Frank built. The fifteen thousand-plus square foot, white stucco ocean-front estate came complete with a tennis court, helicopter pad and pool house, which Jack had taken over. Jack's mother redecorated the home before she died, adding Italian marble floors and mahogany molding. She had impeccable taste, Jack remembered.

Jack was handsome. He was not the model type but he definitely had something – charm – a presence. He was tall and lean, with just *the* right amount of flair. Jack was very much aware of the charm he had on people. The expensive clothes and the cars didn't matter to him, but he was not opposed to his comfortable lifestyle, either. Jack immediately looked at the clock, hurried to dress and headed toward the door, reluctantly, to meet with the professor.

He bent down to pet Haley. "All right girl, you've got security detail."

Haley barked and red lasers appeared from every angle of the room. Jack looked at Haley.

"On second thought, just lock the doors" Jack said, shaking his head at Haley.

THE POWER

CHAPTER FOUR

Jack entered the Professor's classroom as the other students were leaving. He bumped into Adam at the door. "Hmm ... you look like my best friend, Jack, but *he* usually blows off classes until finals – what gives?" Adam asked, jokingly as he elbowed Jack in the arm.

"Uh huh, funny – you're very funny. Please remind me, how *great* the chess club is on your social life," Jack mocked.

"Hey, there is nothing wrong with chess. It involves highly-complicated strategies and skills. There are complex problem-solving maneuvers, brainpower…and…"

But Jack was no longer listening to Adam – he was busy looking at the equivalent of a sunset for the first time ... a dream. Only he was not a dreamer, this was new. His eyes gazed upon Sarah London. Jack shook himself back to reality and regained his composure.

"Who is that?"

Jack mouthed the words to Adam, but he didn't wait for an answer. Intrigue washed away decorum and modesty, giving way to a powerful magnetic pull. He walked toward her and introduced himself.

"I'm Jack Prince," he said, extending his hand.

Sarah shook Jack's hand, politely. She thought for a second that she felt an electrical shock, but casually explained it away. Their brief touch brought to mind images of wedding pictures and family photographs. It was all quite silly, Sarah reasoned. She had never been one to get caught up in whimsical fantasies. "Silliness," she breathed. In reality, no time had passed and Sarah didn't miss a beat with her response.

"I'm Professor Sarah London, she announced. "You're the Jackson Prince that has missed most of the semester and is dangerously close to failing my class."

"Please, call me Jack," he said, ignoring her last statement.

"*Your* class, but I thought Professor Gray"....

"Professor Gray is on leave. This is now *my* class," Sarah interrupted.

"Well, I am very good with tests, I don't anticipate a problem with the exam," Jack said smugly.

"There is a project due today, which you would have known about if you had bothered coming to class; so if I were you, I would get busy Mr. Prince. The project is due by the end of the day," she informed Jack, shoving the assignment instructions into his hand.

"Reproduce an energy saving project utilizing your own creative theory."

Jack read the instructions out loud.

"Uh, yeah…sure, I am totally prepared. Give me one minute."

He quickly surveyed the room for items needed to build an energy model. He took several items from various locations in the classroom to recreate his version of a self–contained energy source without using a battery.

"While this has not been tested … the key to electricity is the movement of electrons."

Jack explained his theory while he worked.

"You simply add a saltwater solution and two types of metals. The atoms carry a positive or negative electric charge. Now, use the addition of a very special alloy in the mix and … let there be light!" Jack exclaimed.

Sarah stared at him, momentarily at a loss for words. Was he for real?

"Assuming you can later submit a paper to support your model, you get an 'A' on the project," Sarah smiled as she packed her briefcase, fumbling nervously.

Jack was not ready for the conversation to be over. He began to feel regret. He suddenly realized that he'd been missing out on something greatly resembling lightning striking. He was certain of one thing; he wanted Sarah London in his life.

"If I had known you were teaching this class, I would never have missed a day," he said smiling. "And call me Jack, please."

Sarah stared blankly at Jack for a minute, not immediately sure of what to say. He seemed overly-confident and a bit smug. He was inappropriately familiar, she assessed.

"I'm your teacher, that–is–all," Sarah said in an authoritative manner. "You're not making the best impression, Mr. Prince. If this is your attempt at being charming, you have failed. Work on your attendance, instead of trying to work on me."

"Can't I do both?" Jack asked, and then took a moment to look Professor London over from head to toe, wanting to remember everything about her. He was having fun trying to unnerve her. He couldn't remember ever having this effect on a girl. "Did I mention I play the guitar?"

"Goodbye, Mr. Prince," Sarah said, with a hint of frustration. She walked away without looking back.

"Hello," Jack said, answering his cell phone.

"Jack, this is Agent Lacy Powell. I am sorry to have to tell you this, but your father is missing. He was meeting with a former agent we suspected of selling stolen technology oversees. I'm not supposed to be telling you this. Personally, I'm not sure what Frank was working on; only that it was based on his research for a new energy source."

"Who was he meeting?" Jack asked. "Do you have a name?"

"Jack, I can't give you specifics and the last thing I need is you going off by yourself, getting into trouble. We were tracking him but we lost transmission and I was hoping that he said something to you before he left that could help us find him?"

"No – he only mentioned the meeting was happening, but my dad never told me the name of a person. I can't help you," Jack answered.

"If you think of anything else, please let me know. I will be in touch."

"Okay, but I hope you don't expect me to sit at home and wait for a phone call."

"I was hoping there was something you could tell us. I didn't call you so that you would run off and do something stupid. Frank had been working alone. There were only a few people in the agency who even knew about the meeting. He wanted to keep the project on a need–to–know–basis," Agent Powell explained.

"Where was the meeting?" Jack asked.

"I don't know and if I did, I am not sure that I could tell you. These people could be after you, too, if they connect the dots."

This didn't make sense, Jack thought. There had to be something more than what Agent Powell was saying. He knew that his dad would have left clues – a trail to follow. Frank had been in danger more times than even Jack knew, but this was the first time the Agency had ever called. Agent Powell seemed worried – it wasn't anything she said … it was more what she wouldn't say.

"Wow, I appreciate your help," Jack said, sarcastically.

"Jack, we will handle this. We will get him back," Agent Powell promised.

"Yeah, like you had my mother's back," he accused. "*I'm* going after him. Personally, I couldn't care less what you think," Jack fired the words off before he disconnected the call. He replayed the conversation in his head –the things he said shocked him. "*I'm going after him,*" he repeated to himself. He didn't know where that came from. It was like he pulled the words out of thin air – he was running on auto–pilot.

Jack drove home and went immediately to his father's office. He began sifting through the desk for any indication as to what his dad was working on. He was certain his dad would have left clues – he was sure of it.

Reading the papers proved more difficult than he anticipated.

Everything was coded with symbols and weird notes. His brain was on overload. *He was so distracted that he didn't even hear the front door open.*

"I let myself in. Dude, what happened to you at school?" Adam asked, interrupting Jack's train of thought. "Professor London is hot, isn't she? I call dibs."

"Adam, I've just received a message about my dad. He may have been kidnapped. It's strange, I know, but I've got to do something." Jack ignored Adam's earlier comments.

"Yeah, like call the police," Adam responded.

"You're kidding right?" Jack asked incredulously. "What should I tell the police? Hmm, my dad, who is a Black Ops Special Agent over Area 58, disappeared. Only a small list of people even know about Black Ops and the police are not on the list. Plus, I watch enough cop TV to know that he has to be missing for at least forty-eight hours before they will do anything.

"Fine," Adam said. "Wait, you mean Area 51, right?"

"No, I mean Area 58," Jack said. "Area 51 is a remote detachment of an Air Force military base used for the purpose of development of experimental weapons – at least that's the unofficial report. The restricted air space surrounding the field makes it the subject of conspiracy theories," Jack grimaced. "Area 58 is a unit within a unit, beyond the reach of most governmental and military departments. Its main purpose has been energy and fuel. People are still freaking out over Area 51 – think of the panic if they knew about Area 58," Jack said.

"So, there really is an Area 51?" Adam asked.

"I can't confirm or deny its existence – it's not something the Agency officially acknowledges," Jack said.

"Fine ... because it's on a need to know basis?" Adam asked.

"Yes," Jack said.

"So, there is an Area 51?" Adam wanted to know.

Jack sighed and put his head down on the desk.

"Forget it," Adam said. "I'm confused. This seems way out of my league here. I'm not sure what I can do. We have so little information to go on. This is completely beyond the realm of possible things that I could imagine happening. It's not part of my world," Adam said.

"Yeah, well ... welcome to my world," Jack answered.

"Listen, isn't there someone in the division that Frank trusted?" Adam asked. "Who would he contact if he was in trouble?"

"Me – he trusted me, or at least he used to," Jack said quietly. "What do you think I should do?"

"*You* are asking *me*? What do I know about any of this?" Adam asked, pacing the floor. "I play chess ... I'm the computer guy. This is secret spy stuff – like a scene from a James Bond movie. I don't understand what you want from me."

"You are my best friend ... you're the advanced mathematics expert who found an error on the mathematics reference table. Your findings are now published in the *Mathematics Education Journal*. In my opinion, that's pretty impressive. You're studying robotic engineering and in every gifted class there is dealing with chemical engineering," Jack insisted.

"Okay," Adam paused. "But from the looks of this, we're going to need help from a few people I know."

"What do you mean?" Jack asked, leaning over Adam's shoulder to look at the computer screen.

"Jack, do you have any clue as to what your dad was working on? Oh, yeah, that's right...you sleep all day and play the guitar all night," Adam reverted back to sarcasm to lighten the tension.

"It's like I always say, chicks dig the guitar." Jack tried to do the same.

"Right ... well, look at this. It's a new energy source of some sort, made of an alloy I don't recognize and the equations are cryptic, but it appears to be a biodegradable fuel source – the same kind that the EPA has been lobbying the government for funding. Russia, China and Japan have all tried to get their hands on this information."

"What secret am I missing?" Jack asked. "What's so dangerous about that?"

"Well, it looks like maybe someone wants to use this as a way to fuel ... a bomb or similar type of chemical weapon."

"Yeah, I knew my dad patented a solar-cell battery. He and my mom presented the findings to the Agency. They found out it was unstable and discontinued the contract. They did not want to risk anyone else working on the prototype. My dad does not make weapons," Jack argued.

"I believe you ... but someone wants him to," Adam said.

Jack's phone rang. He answered but only heard random beeping and then it stopped almost as soon as it started. Jack disconnected the call but, it rang again, followed by the same beeping. "It's nothing," Jack said, dismissing the beeps.

"Wait!" Adam shouted. "Play that back ... those aren't random beeps – it's Morse code!"

"Of course," Jack acknowledged. "My dad and I used to send each other secret messages when I was little using Morse code. I forgot all about that."

Adam translated the message and wrote down the words on a sheet of paper. "It says *sector twelve*. Do you know what that means?"

"I know they are bad news. I remember my dad talking to some of the agents about them – they were trying to get information against them for acts against the government," Jack answered.

"Are you kidding me?" Adam asked. "We are so far over our heads. This is too much. Who knows what we're up against?"

"It doesn't matter what they're after because they are not going to get it. I'm going after them. With your help, we can figure this out together. I will bet on my inherent *know-how* and overall good looks and your brain any day of the week. Isn't that what they called you in high school, 'the Brain?' Jack teased. "Adam, I don't have a lot of options here. You know I will do this alone ... but, I don't have to?"

"We're not comic book characters. This could be dangerous and we could get seriously hurt or worse ... killed."

"Let's make sure that doesn't happen, okay?" Jack said. "My dad's last entry shows a meeting this morning at a coffee shop outside of town. Are you coming?"

He grabbed some notes from the desk and took the keys to the Lamborghini and left. Adam followed.

Jack stood outside the coffee shop and noticed the camera monitoring the entrance. "Adam, I'll talk to the employees while you look in the back for the camera feed. You can use this portable device to download the video."

Inside, Jack questioned the employees and showed them a picture of his father. He spoke to the manager, Cliff, to distract him while Adam went to the back office. "Do you remember seeing this man in your shop this morning?" *He held up a picture he printed from Haley's data bank. It was recorded from earlier today.*

"Yeah, he was in here earlier –he didn't stay long. He ordered coffee, but didn't drink it. When I looked around, he was gone."

"Did you notice if he was with anyone? Did anything seem out of the ordinary – like he was in trouble or agitated?" Jack asked.

"There was nothing out of the ordinary. It's been a slow morning, but I remember that he left with two other gentlemen – can't be for sure. They all left at the same time," Cliff said.

"Can you describe them?"

"Not really. They had on dark suits, but again, I can't be sure. I only remember him because he kept asking me what time it was. He asked once when he came in and then twice while he sat at the table. I wouldn't easily forget him – kept bugging me." The manager admitted.

"Do you remember where the gentleman sat?" Jack asked the manager.

The manager showed Jack the table. He inspected the area, including looking underneath the table and chairs, hoping to find something to help. Jack was certain that his dad would find a way to get a message to him. It was his job to keep his eyes open. Jack felt sick to his stomach over the whole thing. They may not have been close, but he was going to let anything happen to his dad. Jack looked up to see Adam exiting the back office. He distracted the manager until Adam was outside.

"Did you find the camera?" Jack asked.

"Yeah, of course I found the camera. This is *me* you're talking to. I downloaded it, let's go," Adam said, hurriedly.

Once they were clear of the coffee shop, Adam and Jack looked at the video. They watched Frank being forcibly escorted out of the coffee shop, surrounded by four men in dark-colored suits. They couldn't make out the license plate from the angle of the SUV. The men had on dark suits and dark glasses. When the video finally stopped, there was only silence.

"Jack, are you sure about this?" Adam asked.

"I'm all he's got. I know he'd say not to come after him, but he knows that I wouldn't listen to him anyway."

"Look, even with the both of us, we are going to need more brain power. Come on, I know where we might get some help," Adam said, surrendering.

Jack drove the yellow Lamborghini well over the speed limit. He blasted the radio, singing along to the tunes.

"Why do you keep looking back?" Adam yelled over the music.

"I think we are being followed. There is a black SUV that has been tailing us ever since we left the coffee shop," Jack said.

"Followed ... We're being followed? Are you sure?" Adam asked, looking over his shoulder.

"There's only one way to find out. Let them try to follow this," Jack said, as he floored the gas pedal and made a sharp right turn across two lanes of traffic.

"They're still following us," Adam shouted nervously. He turned down the volume on the radio.

"They're getting closer. Speed up or do something!"

"Well, we know one thing – that we are definitely being followed," Jack said.

"Who would be following us? This is not happening – it can't be happening ... Jack, tell me this isn't happening. "

Jack made another sharp turn and ran a red light. The black SUV mimicked his moves and followed suit.

"Adam, I hate to be the voice of reason, but this *is* really happening."

"Stop patronizing me – it's not funny! What are we going to do now?" Adam asked.

"I'm thinking," he said, weaving in and out of traffic. "Okay ... I have an idea."

"I'm listening."

"Let's see how good you really are at this game," Jack smirked.

He reached in the back seat and handed Adam the remote control airplane. Adam caught on quickly. He leaned out the window and took aim. He fired a series of darts which hit the SUV's tires.

"Bingo!" Adam shouted.

The SUV swerved sideways and ran off the road, crashing into the side of a building.

"What do you think they were after?" Adam asked.

"I don't know and I don't plan to stick around to find out," Jack shouted.

"We're going to the University. Let's take the North exit," Adam said.

"What are those papers?"

"It's a map of a non-existent place," Adam said. These dots are scattered across the page in a type of pattern, but I haven't been able to determine what it means. The dots are placed too specifically to be random."

"You're right. I doubt it's random – we just have to find the key. The symbol at the top of the page represents Sector Twelve," Jack explained.

"*What or who* is Sector Twelve?"

"Sector Twelve is a private conglomerate of former military and government personnel. Most have ties to the CIA and FBI on a consulting basis. They call themselves Sector Twelve; the name is based on biblical writings about the twelve Hebrew tribes of Israel. They see themselves as saviors of the nation. From what my dad said about them, I believe they want domination and world power and they're not really picky about the means by which they get that power," Jack said.

"What do they plan to do with all the power?" Adam asked.

"Rule the world, of course. Their goal is to control the nation's money and resources. The map is divided into twelve quadrants. Each quadrant is controlled by one of the twelve agents, but it's nearly impossible to determine which agent is associated with each region without the code key."

"Well, I need answers fast. So ... what do you have in mind?"

"That's why we're here. Follow me," Adam told Jack.

Jack walked the familiar university halls. Adam waved impatiently, trying to hurry him along. Jack had passed this building before – it was the music auditorium theater. Only students with a musical curriculum would have reason to be here. Music could be heard coming from inside. They opened the doors, to reveal a girl standing on the stage, playing a violin. Her olive skin was flawless. She had straight black hair that was pulled into a high ponytail. She looked more like a senior in high school than a college student, neatly attired in dark denim jeans, argyle vest and converse tennis shoes. Jack instantly recognized the musical number. It was Niccolo Paganini's *Caprice No. 23* in A minor.

"Guys, this is a closed practice. I have the auditorium for another hour," she said.

"Ivy, this is Jack Prince. Jack, Ivy Cannon."

"Adam, whatever it is that you're going to ask me, the answer is no!"

"Look – we have a problem and I thought maybe you could help us?" Adam walked across the stage, stumbling, barely missing the hole in the floor, reserved for the orchestra pit.

"Ivy is music major but she has equally impressive skills," Adam whispered to Jack.

"Adam, stop sucking up – what do you want this time?" Ivy asked. "Whatever it is, my answer is still *no* – you always manage to get me into trouble."

"Did I mention you get to beat people up?" Adam teased.

"Oh, well that changes everything. Why didn't you start with that? I'm in," Ivy said, smiling.

"You're kidding me, right? Did I miss the punch line? I'm sure you're a tough girl, but just because you can beat up Adam, doesn't mean that you can hold your own with someone twice your size. Besides, *he's* kind of soft around the middle," Jack's laughter filled the room.

"I'm a double major in music and advanced mathematics. I speak five languages and if that's not enough, I'm a Master Black Belt in Jujitsu and Karate."

Ivy quickly took a defensive stance. Before Jack realized what was happening, Ivy spun around in the air and landed on one leg. She kicked the violin stand, splitting it in half, sending the pole spiraling into the wall, narrowly missing Jack's head. The move was graceful yet terrifying, reminiscent of martial arts icon, Bruce Lee. "That move is called, *the Roadhouse*," Ivy said, smirking.

Jack raised his hands in the air with his palms facing forward. He looked at Ivy with his mouth gaped open. He wasn't sure if he should applaud or duck for cover. She was definitely unexpected and jaw-dropping, Jack thought.

"Extraordinary … you're in!"

"Of course, I am," Ivy said, confidently. "What am I *in*, actually?"

"We'll fill you in later," Adam said. "Take your car and follow us – we have one more stop."

Once inside the car, Jack fired off questions about Ivy. Adam met her a year ago for the first time when he attempted to rescue her from a guy who was being hyper-aggressive and brash. He quickly found that she could handle herself. She broke two of the guy's ribs. He saw her again when she attended a few of the chess club meetings. They shared a similar group of friends and he would see her around campus. They became friends after he attended a symphony in the music hall. That was the day he discovered Ivy was both cerebral and a masterful musician. They had a few study sessions together after that and he credited her with helping him pass French class.

"We're here," Adam said, with excitement.

"Where are we exactly? Is this someone's garage or a mechanic shop?" Jack asked.

"Honestly … it's a little of both – you'll see," Adam said. "Come on."

They walked past several vintage modeled cars. Jack slowed to a crawl as he admired an orange colored, mint condition 1969 Pontiac GTO. Adam pointed to the man leaning over the engine of one of the cars. The man had his back toward them and didn't appear to notice their arrival.

"Is this guy necessary?" Jack sighed, looking at his watch.

"You tell me."

Adam picked up a wrench and threw it toward the man's head. Even though he had his back toward them, he raised his hand and caught the wrench, as if on cue.

"Didn't your mother ever tell you not to throw things, Adam?"

"Finch, can you take some time off? I think you're going to like this … let's call it an assignment."

Jack looked intently at the man. He moved closer and stood within inches of him, waving his hand in front of the man's eyes. "You're blind!" Jack exclaimed.

"Wow, did you figure that out all by yourself," the man scoffed.

"Finch, this is Jack Prince – he's why I'm here," Adam said.

Finch picked up an apple from his work shelf. He tossed the apple in the air, then picked up a bowie knife and threw it with expert precision, pinning the apple to the wall.

"I'm sorry, it's just that I haven't met many blind mechanics," Jack said.

"Yes, I believe that, but I'm not a mechanic. I'm a software engineer that likes to fix cars because it relaxes me. I can fix anything and break into anything. What can I say — I'm good with my hands. Wanna test me on that, honey?" Finch said, looking in Ivy's direction.

"How did you know she was standing there?" Jack asked.

"You smell like Christmas morning!" Finch answered, never taking his eyes off Ivy.

"She's a babe, am I right?" He smiled. "I'm right, aren't I?"

"The babe's name is Ivy Cannon," Adam said.

"Your name is Finch … Finch, what? Do you have a last name?" Jack asked.

"Who are you, the IRS?" Finch asked. "Is this an interrogation?"

"This will work. It's just his brand of humor – you'll get used to him," Adam answered Jack's exasperated sigh. "Finch, do you still have your contacts at the Agency? We need information fast and we're going to need your help on the inside to get what we need."

"Is this legal?" Finch asked.

"Does that matter?" Jack questioned.

"I like to know what I'm getting myself into," Finch smiled. "You should know that my services are not free."

"Name your price … money won't be a problem." Jack said.

"Now, you're speaking my language — I'm in," Finch laughed.

"If Adam vouches for you, that's good enough for me, no matter how successfully opinionated and self-absorbed."

"Are we exchanging measurements, here? Then you should know that I will take the *assignment* on Adam's word, even though you make a bad first impression as a spoiled, over-indulgent rich kid who's never worked a day in his life and is used to people catering to his every whim." Finch smiled.

"You're quick. I like that," Jack said.

"He's more than that. Among other things, he's been on his own since age sixteen — he put himself through college. He has more post graduate degrees than anyone I know. He is nationally recognized for his research on sound wave vibrations. He would never admit it, but he's a self-made millionaire and has offers from every university around for a post. He is genuine," Adam argued.

"Hey, all this praise will go to my head. Can I ride with the babe?" Finch asked as he followed Ivy to her car.

"How does he do that?" Jack asked, staring after Finch.

"Later" Adam smiled, patting Jack on the back. "Let's go."

CHAPTER FIVE

Frank arrived at the coffee shop early. He wanted to have plenty of time to prepare before the meeting. He looked around the room for his contact — but he didn't appear to be present, so he waited. He was supposed to meet a man named Lincoln, under the pretense of buying a special–made metal, some overseas groups had been using to make weapons. He didn't know who, but someone had stolen his designs — designs that he had developed for an energy source that were now being used to make weapons; and he was going to get to the bottom of it.

"Are you Frank Prince?" The man in the black suit asked.

"We spoke over the phone, I'm Lincoln."

Behind him, three other men sat down at opposite tables nearby. Lincoln gestured for Frank to stand, "If you please put your hands out. You can never be too careful. You are not wearing a wire are you?"

After Lincoln and his men were fully satisfied that Frank was not wired, they sat down. Soon after sitting down, Lincoln received a phone call that increasingly agitated him. *Something is off*, Frank thought. He heard Lincoln say something about collecting the package, as ordered. He didn't like the delivery of his words.

"Everything is going according to plan. We will make the delivery as scheduled."

"This is not going to end well," Frank said under his breath.

Frank tried to end the meeting quickly.

"If this is a bad time…"

"No, the time is perfect. I understand you're interested in purchasing some metal. Because you come with high recommendation, the price will be discounted. It will only cost *you* five million US dollars," Lincoln explained.

Frank had a sixth sense kicked in; he had minutes to make a decision to keep himself from being kidnapped or killed. He sent several messages to Agent Powell and to Jack, hoping that one of them would be able to decode it. He was stalling.

Jack is clever and capable of more than he realized. I hate to put Jack in the middle of this, but right now, he's my best hope. I'd stake my life on it any day of the week.

"Mr. Prince, you don't look well; perhaps we should step outside for some air. We can finish talking about our business there. Would you join us?" Lincoln said, standing.

"We could always go after your son, Jack and get what we're looking for from him. Isn't that his name?" Lincoln asked, leaning closer to Frank, when he didn't answer.

"Leave him out of this! You'll regret it, I promise you, if he is harmed in any way," Frank said. "He's not a part of this … just leave him alone."

"We will as long as you come with us," Lincoln said.

Frank walked out of the coffee shop, followed by Lincoln and the other men. There was a black van parked in front of the exit. He felt something sting his neck and reached his hand to his neck. The last thing he remembered was collapsing as everything went dark. The men pushed Frank into the van and drove away.

CHAPTER SIX

"What are we doing here exactly?" Ivy asked, following Jack into his father's office.

Haley barked and growled at the guests. She paced back and forth between Ivy and Finch, snarling and bearing her teeth.

"Calm down, girl. They're friends — be good," Jack said, patting her on the head. "She gets jealous but she's harmless."

"She looks hungry. Has she ever bitten anyone?" Ivy asked.

"You don't have to worry about a thing, as long as I'm here. I'll protect you," Finch said, as he placed his hand on Ivy's shoulder.

"Big mistake," Adam breathed.

"I ... don't ... like ... to ... be ... touched," Ivy said, dragging out every word.

Before anyone knew what was happening, she grabbed Finch's hand and flipped him on his back. He lay on the ground, looking up at her, open-mouthed and dazed.

"That was unexpected. I like that," he said.

"Guys, this is Haley. She's harmless," Jack said, pointing the remote at Haley. Her eyes flashed bright yellow; she then walked over and sat underneath the table.

"Okay — that's very cool," Ivy said. "Stay," Ivy said quietly.

"Haley is a robot of sorts... her use has never been tested really. She is one big computer chip, infused with a camera, and a ton of data," Jack explained.

"I think you should explain why we're here," Adam said, impatiently.

Jack turned and faced everyone. He cleared his throat and spoke in a serious tone. "My dad is Frank Prince. He is a highly-specialized engineer."

He is also an ex–government agent, turned consultant. His title would be Black Ops division — I don't expect you to know what that means … no one does. His latest projects have made him a target for groups seeking world-wide power. He is working with the EPA on a biodegradable fuel source utilizing a new type of metal, specifically an alloy to be used in generators. Imagine a battery that never needs charging, that never dies. The possibilities are endless and there are some people that will pay billions to get their hands on his work. Someone is using his designs to make weapons. This morning, my dad went to a meeting and never came back. We're going to find him."

"Is anyone else thinking that you're crazy? Because that's what I'm thinking … you're crazy and – well, we must be crazy, too," Ivy said, as she wandered around the room, picking up items like a kid in a candy store. There were so many gadgets and curious inventions that made her want to know more, but she was deliberately cautious.

"My vote is with the babe… this is wild," Finch said, winking in Ivy's direction.

"Please, stop calling me that!" She said, with an intended warning.

"Guys, let's get serious. Jack, where do we start?" Adam asked, clapping his hands to get their attention.

"Wait — look at this," Jack said. "Someone is downloading information from the computer. They are copying the files right under our noses."

"Move over," Adam said, pushing Jack out of the way. "Well … I can't reverse it, but I can stop them from getting any more than what they've already got. Basically, I'm creating an impenetrable lock box and moving everything to the hidden compartment, where it's secure," he said. "Somebody is trying to get information, dude, and a lot of it. Hopefully, we put a stop to it."

"Do you have any idea who is behind this?" Jack asked.

"That's what we're going to find out," Adam said.

Everyone looked up as the doorbell rang. Jack pointed the remote to Haley. Her eyes flashed and she stood up.

"Who's at the door, girl?" He asked, pushing more buttons on the remote.

Haley's eyes flashed images of the visitors.

"She's connected to the cameras," Jack whispered. "Her eyes act as a type of projector. It's Agent Powell and two other impatient looking agents."

"Ivy, make yourself useful and hide these folders. We don't want them to get anything, if we can help it. They'll be looking for information. Adam, download as many files as you can. I'm going to stall them at the door for as long as I can. Finch ... do whatever it is that you do. Something tells me they weren't just in the neighborhood," Jack said grimacing.

"What have I gotten myself into," Ivy asked, hiding the files in her jacket. "I just hope we don't end up on *America's Most Wanted* for tampering with evidence."

"Hello," Jack said, once he'd opened the door. "What brings you here?"

"We are working diligently on Frank's case. Have you heard anything?" Agent Powell asked.

"Have you?" Jack countered.

"I asked you first," she said. "Are you deliberately being evasive?"

"This is my father we're talking about and I *thought* your friend. Are you really going to stand there and tell me that you don't know anything?" Jack shouted.

"Can we come in and discuss this?" Agent Powell asked.

"I will be happy to invite you in when it's more convenient, I have friends visiting at the moment."

"This is not a game, Jack. I don't want to arrest you for hindering the investigation, but I will if you get in my way. I have a warrant, so I don't need your permission. I'm going to have to insist that you step aside so we can get Frank's computer."

"Fine ... since I can't stop you — come in," Jack shouted, loud enough for Adam and the others to hear them coming.

"Who do we have here?" Agent Powell asked.

"We're friends," Ivy said.

"What's your name?" The agent asked her.

"This is not good," Adam breathed. He put his head down. "Um…she doesn't respond well to authority. She has attitude five times her small frame – that's a warning."

"What's your name, girl?" The agent repeated.

"Are *you* talking to me? Are *you* talking to me?" Ivy said, in her best Robert DeNiro accent. The agent put his hand on Ivy's shoulder and the mood of the room shifted.

"Too late," Adam whispered.

Ivy grabbed the man's hand and maneuvered herself around him so that she had his arm behind his back.

"Touch me again and I will break it, beyond repair," Ivy said,

"I do believe the lady means what she says," Finch said, standing next to her.

Ivy looked at Finch. It was the first time she really looked at him. He was about her height, with sun-bronzed colored hair. He was handsome, toned and sculpted, but he was the "trying to look like he was not trying too hard" type. He was neat and clean. His black T-shirt and dark jeans smelled freshly laundered and his nails were manicured. Finch was a fraud. He could not be as big a jerk as he was pretending to be. Ivy laughed at the thought.

"I think you have what you came here for, so I am asking you to leave," Jack said.

"I *will* be in touch," Agent Powell said. "Don't leave town — we may have more questions for you. Please know that we are doing everything we can to find Frank. You can help by going about your normal routine and staying out of our way."

Everyone was quiet until the agents left. They sat still until the door was shut and Jack re-entered the room.

"You watch too many movies," he said, laughing at Ivy.

"What can I say? I'm a movie buff. *Taxi Driver* is a classic. I have always wanted to say that. I couldn't help myself," she said, putting her head down into her hands.

"All right guys, let's get back to work," Jack said.

"I have an idea," Adam began explaining.

"Shh," Finch gestured with his finger to hush everyone. "I'm hungry. I vote for pizza," he said walking around the room, looking underneath tables and chairs. He reached underneath the desk and found a listening device and smashed it on the floor. "That makes three pepperoni pizzas, two pineapple pizzas and one cheese pizza," he shouted, leaning into Ivy. He turned the lamp upside down and removed a second device, stomping on it with his shoe. He placed the remnants of the devices into a bag and tossed them into the trash.

"We should be fine now. All the bugs are gone – this house is clean," Finch smiled.

"How did you know they bugged the room?" Jack smiled, looking out the window.

"I bet the agents are disappointed. I can't read lips, but I don't think they're saying very nice things about us. They're parked in a van across the street, and now they're driving away."

Jack faced Finch, gazing intently.

"You *are* handy to have around. How did you know?" he repeated.

"I have hearing that would make superman jealous," Finch smirked, leaning back on the sofa. "It's the frequency mostly, and their movements seemed way too calculated. Once they were out the door, I heard a high frequency pitch from the two devices; it's not rocket science."

"I have another portable computer, several others, actually," Jack said, hooking the cables to the spare computer.

"We can download the files you copied and keep looking for clues."

"Do you know what you're doing?" Adam asked.

"No … not really," Jack admitted quietly. "But I'm a quick study."

"Ok, listen, this is dangerous. We don't know how far these guys will go to get what they want. Maybe we should listen to Agent Powell and stay put," Adam said.

"I need to know if you're in this or not…you can leave, no questions asked," Jack said. "I'm not in denial about the difficulty of what I'm asking. Yes, it's crazy and unfathomable; we are probably in over our heads – but I am going after my dad, alone if I have to. What would you do in my position?"

"Can we order pizza?" Finch asked.

"What — you're asking about food," Jack responded with sarcasm.

"I'm hungry," Finch said, shrugging his shoulders.

"Yes. We can most definitely order pizza. Order anything you want – I'm paying," Jack said.

"I'm in," Finch said.

"I'm in, too," said Ivy. "I want chicken, cheese and tomato on my pizza."

Everyone looked at Adam. He was the only one who had not spoken. "It's unanimous. Of course, I'm in."

CHAPTER SEVEN

Jack walked over to the bookshelves. He removed the tallest book with the green and gold foil binding and quickly replaced it. When the book was replaced, a hidden entrance opened to reveal an even larger room, tucked away behind the shelves.

It looked like a command center for some comic book superhero. It was much too business-like to be cozy, with metal objects, blinking lights, boxes and tools. The centerpiece was a huge supercomputer, comparable to any of those used by national security agencies with global surveillance.

There was an oversized concrete desk with monitor screens on both ends. A mechanized workshop area and vast library covered the west side wall. There was a kitchen and oversized leather sofa on the north end of the room to complete the high-tech facility.

"Is your dad Batman or something? This is like the top secret Bat cave!" Ivy said.

"It's just a workshop," Jack said, trying to restrain his laughter. "My dad usually hides out for hours in here when designing prototypes. As you can imagine, he does a lot of research."

"I will spread the papers here, so that you can look at them together. We are looking for information on my dad's energy project and for anyone interested in purchasing it. If you see something that looks out of place, let me know," Jack said. "This particular document is a map covering Sector Twelve. The randomly patterned dots are representative of something ... I just haven't been able to figure that part out yet," he whispered.

"I will see what I can find on the computer," Adam said. "The area is much too broad to decipher without a key code of some sort. Maybe I can find something in his files."

Jack picked up his guitar and started strumming a tune. He sat on the corner of the sofa near where Ivy was seated. She applauded vigorously while he played. She started humming the melody.

"I've got it!" Ivy shouted, slapping Jack on the back.

She ran to stand over the map, banging her hand on the table, repeatedly.

"I think I know the key," she said with excitement. "These are not dots ... they are musical notes. That's the key code," she explained. "You can see that the black dots, depending on their location on the page, represent a musical note. If you lay the map on top of this bar, you can figure out what the dots are trying to tell us."

"Gold star for the lady," Jack said.

"From an initial search, the names appear to be weapon dealers. They buy sell and trade weapons. These guys are after one thing only ... power," Adam said. "I'm guessing whoever has the biggest weapon has the most power."

"If its weapons, they want then by all means, let's accommodate them," Jack said intensely as he began building various mechanical-like weapons, moving in one of those faster than light frenzies.

"These guys are bad news and we're going in there *with tinker toys*?" Adam asked, sarcastically. "I don't think they're going to be very impressed with us!"

Adam picked up one of the gadgets Jack made and threw it at the wall. An explosion blasted a hole in the wall and knocked them off their chairs.

"It will work ... trust me," Jack said.

"Can you warn a guy, next time?" Finch joked. "I can help. What do you want me to do?"

"The more hands, the better."

I will hand you several oval shaped compartments. All you have to do is insert these liquid gel sacs and snap them shut. You will know it's securely tight when the textured ridges lay smooth. Whatever you do don't drop them. They're the equivalent of gas bombs. Ivy, you can pack them in the bags, once he's finished."

"How do you know how to do all this?" Ivy asked. "We're here because of our unique gifts, I get that much. What's your talent ... your gift?"

"I don't know that I've ever thought of it that way. I remember things. Actually, I remember everything I've ever seen, heard or read, even if for a second. My photographic memory is why I am able to pass classes without actually attending, I suppose."

"And what else?" Ivy asked.

"What do you mean, *what else?*"

"Haven't you noticed that you sometimes move faster than the average person? Someone with your type of mind gift may have similar mind gifts that deal with moving objects," she said.

"No, I haven't noticed," Jack said.

"It's just a theory. Time will tell, I suppose."

"I'm sorry to interrupt your teaching segment," Finch said, sarcastically. "But what does this contraption do? I can feel an independent heat source inside."

"That design is one of my dad's original prototypes. It's like a laser gun, but the bullets are a blended alloy that liquefies on contact. It will shock the system ... more like electrocute, but it won't kill you. It is extremely painful, however. You will wish for death. You won't be able to move for hours," Jack explained. "It's also safe on the environment – the whole thing is biodegradable."

"That's good to know," Ivy laughed. "Ropes ... check. Gas bombs ... check. Poison tip darts coated with a numbing agent ... check. Liquefying death-rays ... check. I think that's everything," she announced.

"The message we received earlier traced back to coordinates near a military base. There is a plant there where the military stockpiles weapons outside Amarillo, Texas. It's still too large an area to cover but its more information than we had thirty minutes ago.

"We don't have time to guess ... we need to be certain," Jack said.

"I'm doing the best that I can with the information I have. It's going to take a little more time," Adam said, leaning over the computer keys, typing furiously.

"We just may be in luck," Jack said, grabbing his keys.

"Tell us what the big mystery is," Ivy said.

"I will be back as soon as I can. I think I know someone else who can get us closer," he said. "It's a long shot, but if I can pull this off, it will give us a huge advantage. I may know someone who knows someone that can get us closer."

"Don't be long, Jack," Adam warned.

"I'm taking the *McLaren* from the garage."

"Exactly how many cars do you have?" Ivy smiled.

"Remind me to give you a tour of the showcase when we have time," Jack laughed. "By the way, there's plenty of food in the refrigerator and if you have to leave, tell Haley – she knows how to lock up," Jack said, closing the door behind him.

CHAPTER EIGHT

Jack rang the doorbell.

"Hello, what are you doing here?" Professor London asked.

"Wow. There are a thousand and one things that I practiced on the way over here, but it seems I have forgotten them all," Jack said.

"I know this must seem awkward, at least it is for me."

"You can start by telling me why you're here," she repeated.

"It's just that I know the whole thing is going to sound implausible and I'm not sure how to begin," he said.

"Mr. Prince, how do you even know where I live? Are you following me?"

"No, I remember reading it on your I.D. tag, from your briefcase. Can I come in?" Jack smiled politely, waiting for an invitation to enter.

"Is this related to your class assignment? I have posted office hours," she said, talking at a fast pace, not stopping for Jack's reply. "This is highly irregular, Mr. Prince. At first you don't come to class at all and then you show up with questionable manners and now, you appear on my door step unannounced – it's all very unusual."

"Sarah, may I call you Sarah?" Jack jumped into the conversation, when she stopped to breathe.

"No, you may not, Mr. Prince," she responded. "It's best this remains on a professional level – so again, I ask, "What brings you here, Mr. Prince? And please don't tell me that you were in the neighborhood."

In actuality, Jack wanted to tell Sarah that from the moment he saw her – he'd thought of little else. He remembered every inflection of her voice, every word she spoke in their initial meeting, the clothes and color of the makeup she had worn. Had it not been for the unfortunate reason that brought him here, he would have camped out at her place until she sent him home, he thought. Jack wasn't sure what to make of his feelings, but he couldn't deny them. He was almost certain that it would send Sarah running in the other direction if he were bold enough to whisper even a hint of it. It would have to wait until another time. Time meant so much more now – and he didn't feel there was enough of it, at least not where his dad was concerned.

"Actually, I'm here about the tattoo on the inside of your wrist," Jack began slowly.

Sarah looked down at her wrist which was still hidden behind the door. She glared at Jack silently.

"How did you know about my tattoo?" she asked. "What do you know about it?"

"I told you. I remember things…it's the photographic memory. Even without that, I assure you nothing about you is easily forgotten." Jack continued, "It's a military brand, right?"

"Come in," she exhaled.

Jack looked around the house. It was very modern, but cozy and neat … very neat. It was overly organized, with a nautical beach style decor. Nothing was out of place. There were volumes of books, alphabetized and color-coded on the shelves. Same color white flowers were positioned throughout the house. Jack noticed Sarah liked fresh cut flowers and wondered if she had them delivered, since he didn't see a garden. The mail was neatly sorted. Everything was immaculate, right down to the military corners on the bed in the guest room. Jack turned his attention back to Sarah, who was explaining the tattoo.

"The tattoo is mostly in memory of my father. He was in the Air Force. His team all had these tattoos – it was their insignia … their seal. We traveled quite often growing up, not by choice. You have to go where they send you. Don't misunderstand me, -I'm not complaining. It was actually fun most of the time.

He was a pilot at first and quickly increased in rank, becoming a Command Chief Master Sergeant. When he died ... well, it made me feel like he was still around to have a tattoo like his. I know it probably seems silly," she said.

"Professor London, it doesn't sound silly at all," Jack said, quietly.

"You can call me Sarah when we're not in the classroom."

"Are you familiar with a Power Plant outside Amarillo?"

"Now, I'm really curious," Sarah said. "I did some flight training near Sheppard's Air Base in Wichita, Texas not too far from that plant before getting assigned to the Special Weapons Unit. I was only there for a couple of years. Once my father was gone, it just wasn't fun anymore. I decided to get some distance ... so I came here."

"I'm sorry to hear about that – your father, I mean. I know this is going to sound crazy, but I've just learned to go with my instincts about these things," Jack said.

"And what are your instincts telling you about me, precisely?" Sarah asked.

She looked at Jack, leaning her head to one side. He was puzzling. His manner was casual and self–assured, but he wasn't telling her everything. She wanted to press him to find out why he arrived at her door. It was obvious that he could be disciplined and focused, but apparently he was either lazy or didn't care when it concerned college work. She didn't know him well enough to know what his general demeanor was like – was he just trying to impress her?

"My instincts are telling me that you're tough enough to handle what I am about to tell you," Jack said.

They sat down on the oversized pale blue sofa. Jack briefed Sarah on the day's events. Maybe it was her military background that enabled her to take everything in without reacting with shock and speculation...or her calm reaction could have been the result of a class full of over–zealous, gifted college students on their own for the first time. Either way, he was impressed with her apprehension. Jack told Sarah about the events leading up to his visit, about his dad, the apparent kidnapping and how she could help since her background meant she likely had information about the military training facilities. He was sure that her specialized knowledge of the local area would lead him straight to his dad ... or so he was hoping.

CHAPTER NINE

Back at the Prince Family Estate – Adam, Ivy and Finch were busy working to put together a strategy for the rescue. They rummaged through emails, calendar entries, journals, and phone messages. Finch had just hacked into a classified, government database when Jack walked in the door with Professor London. The vibe in the room quickly shifted when they entered. It was a jaw-dropping silence – similar to the way kids stop talking when parents enter the room.

"Who invited the teacher?" Ivy blurted out.

"Professor London …I'm Adam, by the way," Adam mumbled. "Did I miss something, Jack?"

"I know that you all have questions. I can see the shocked looks on your faces … in the case of Ivy, the gaped opening in your mouth is a dead giveaway," Jack said. "I invited Professor London …"

"Sarah – you can call me Sarah," she said.

"As I was saying, I invited *Sarah* because she has information about the military base in Texas. Plus, she can probably help us with determining the best way to get in without being seen," Jack said.

"There's been some miscommunication. I plan on doing much more than that; I'm going with you," Sarah said with assertion.

"No one said anything about you coming with us. I never agreed to that," Jack grimaced.

"You are going to need a pilot – that's number one. Flying is the best way in, if not the only way in, where we're going. There's one road in and out and that road will be heavily watched. I will pilot us there – it's settled," Sarah said. "Adam, I'll need to go over security with you. If they're stockpiling weapons, you'll need all the help you can get."

"No – it's not settled. You are not going with us," Jack said again.

"Come on … isn't that why you came to my house?" Sarah smiled. "Why are you being so disagreeable all of a sudden? You've admitted that I have key information needed for the success of this trip. I know the area better than anyone here and I'm the best pilot around. If you get another pilot, that will require going through proper channels and you'll need to log the flight plan with air traffic control and I'm guessing you don't have that kind of clearance."

"Professor London, will this in any way negatively affect our grade?" Ivy asked, raising her hand. "I don't want to get kicked out of school or anything like that – I'm on a scholarship." "No, Ivy – no need to worry," Sarah reassured her. "I'm pretty sure we would both have to answer for going on this little mission. I'm not going to tell the school board if you don't," she said.

"No one is listening to me. I didn't say you could come with us," Jack said. "It's not that I wouldn't appreciate your company, it's just that this is more than I can ask – more than I should ask of you," he said in a voice that only she could hear. "I don't want this moment in time to be one of your first impressions of me. I don't think I'd forgive myself if something happened before we had a chance to go on a proper date," he spilled out the words clumsily. She hadn't even heard him play the guitar yet, he thought to himself.

"Look Jack, it was your idea to bring *'professor hottie'* here – so, I assume you had good reason. I vote she stays. Besides, if she really does have information on the location, then we're going to need her. It's probably the smartest decision made so far – but I'm just a guest," Finch said in his usual sarcastic tone.

"We've never been properly introduced and you look familiar," Sarah moved closer, waving her hand in front of his face.

Finch glared at her, following her movements with his eyes – then looking her over from head to toe.

"Amazing," Sarah said. "You're blind."

"Yes ... I know," Finch smirked.

"I'm sorry. Of course, you're blind ... but your visual acuity is so precise," she continued talking, while moving her hand up and down in front of his face.

"Please stop doing that," he said. "It's really annoying when people do that. I can't imagine you would like it very much if I did that to you repeatedly."

"Sorry ... again. What did you do – amp up the resonance with a type of motion sensor?" Sarah asked.

"I like to call it a vibrator, but yeah it increases sound waves, translating movement into a language since, as you know, atoms are simply energy."

"I knew that I recognized you," she said, smiling with excitement. "Finch, I read your thesis on sound waves, it was really eloquent and impactful. I know that you received an award for your research, so I was not the only one impressed, obviously – you've achieved major notoriety in your field."

"Teacher's pet," Ivy whispered under her breath.

"Hey, what are you trying to do, Professor? "Do you want to ruin my tough guy reputation?"

"I like her," Finch said to Jack.

"Your thesis changed the way we think about sound waves...I mean the ability to see sound so distinctively – It's brilliant. I would like to know more," Sarah told him, sitting down next to him.

CHAPTER 10

"Hello ... hmm," Jack said, disconnecting the call. The phone immediately rang again.

"Hello ... the line is still open, but no one is there," Jack said.

"I'll see if I can set up a trace. Your dad could be trying to lead you to him," Adam said. "In theory, we can trace it by satellite, it's just a matter of a simple search and a bit of hi–jacking some codes. This may take a while, let's hope the line stays open long enough. I'll call you when I'm ready," Adam said.

Finch and Ivy packed supplies while Jack made extra weapons. Sarah stared at Jack. She suddenly felt like she was in grade school in a weird and inappropriate way since Jack was a student, technically, and she shouldn't be imagining the two of them watching movies or dancing underneath the moonlight. Completely inappropriate, she thought.

"What's your story Jack? How do you see this ending?" She asked. "You're obviously gifted and talented, but you don't go to class. You have a strained relationship with your father, but you're ready to undergo this impossibly dangerous rescue mission with a bunch of inexperienced students. It's crazy, you know?"

"Wow," Jack said, looking at Sarah. "You don't beat around the bush, do you?"

"No, I've never been one to hold back – patience is not one of my virtues," she said.

"Well, yeah – this does seem a bit crazy, I suppose, but I don't believe it's impossible, either. And as to who I am ... I guess I'm still finding that out," Jack responded. "My mother was the glue that bonded our family together and when she died...well, lets' just say, we miss the glue."

My mother would have liked you very much. You both have the same mindset. You have similar temperaments. I think you would have gotten along really well. You say what you mean – that's something my parents would appreciate. It's a rare quality."

"Thank you ... I think," Sarah said.

"It's definitely a compliment," Jack said laughing. "So, it's your turn. What are you doing teaching a classroom? What's your story, since we're playing twenty questions? You are definitely unexpected – not your typical physics professor."

"Oh, that's right," Sarah said. "Professors don't look like me, right?

"Whoa," Jack said, holding his hands in the air. "I'm just asking why? Don't you ever ask yourself why?"

"No, not really. I never ask myself questions I'm not ready to answer," Sarah said.

She wasn't ready to have this conversation, especially when she hadn't decided if she liked him or not. He was simply a student. He was a lazy, procrastinating, neglectful student or at least that was her first impression. But there was more ... the fact that she was willing to follow him around the world, gave her the answers she needed. Jack was exorbitantly rich, but he didn't brag about it – it was just normal for him. He drove *Veyrons*, *McLarens* and *Pagani Zondas* as if they were standard issue. There was a helicopter pad in his back yard and yachts docked in nearby– it was part of the package. He was definitely used to getting what he wanted.

"If you were in my position, what would you do?" Jack asked her.

"If I were in your position ... I would do whatever it takes. I'd do whatever it takes," Sarah said.

"I've found something," Adam yelled. He pulled out the map. "This is where the signal ends. It matches the coordinates we were given, but there is nothing marking it on the map – it's as if nothing is there."

"Here is the Air Force base. Surrounding the base are three training camps. These two circles that I'm drawing represent the training camps – they are not going to be on any map," Sarah said, pointing to the center of the map. "These facilities are mainly for storage," she pointed out. "They are kept under lock and key but not heavily guarded … usually. South of these buildings is a more remote warehouse with cameras at two entry points and there is a hidden underground level, perfect for a hideout because no one is there on a daily basis."

"We are going to need an invisibility cloak or at least manage to disable some wiring from the chopper …we don't want them to see us coming so we need to make sure we're not on radar."

"I can handle that but I need to get some supplies, if I can get a lift back to my place," Finch said.

"I'll drive you – but don't get any ideas," Ivy said.

"Later," Finch waved goodbye.

"Here is a list of the directors of Sector 12 that I decoded. I assume these guys would like to stay hidden. But if you can work your magic on the computer and see what comes up, I'd appreciate it," Jack said.

"That's what I do," Adam said, laughing. "Stand back and give me room …. kids don't try this home," Adam said smugly.

"He's in his element," Sarah told Jack. "He's having fun ... they all are. This is one big adventure to them. I really want things to work out as smoothly as you think they will, Jack … for their sake."

"They know what they're up against," he said.

"No, they don't and neither do you. You can't possibly know. This has the potential to go horribly wrong. That's why I feel the need to go and oversee things. This is not a class field trip. I don't want anything to happen just when I'm beginning to like you so much. I want you to remain safe. I want Frank to be safe, as well."

"Thank you." "What are you going to do after this? What's next?

"Well, Professor…."

"Okay, I think we're way past the point of you calling me professor."

"I was hoping you could help me out with the next part. I'm hoping it includes you," Jack chimed. "Since you're admitting that you're beginning to like us and we like you ... I like you. I would like to spend more time with you when we're not running off on a dangerous mission. You're an intriguing person ...*I'm* intrigued.

"Talk louder, if you don't mind – I don't want to strain my ears trying to hear," Adam shouted from across the room.

Jack threw one of the sofa pillows at Adam, hitting him on the head.

"You've known me one day – not even a full day," Sarah whispered.

"How long do you need?" he asked, reaching for her hand.

"Longer than one day, Jack. After this ... you're going to be my Prince Charming, is that it?" she asked.

"I want to be," he said, staring into her eyes. They sat there for several minutes, trapped in a gaze, until Sarah released his hold and looked away. Jack sank into the chair and began strumming his guitar. He watched Sarah intently as he played.

"I just want to be your everything," he hummed quietly. *"I just want to be your everything."*

Sarah tried to look uninterested, but her heart was melting, betraying her with each passing minute. She was in trouble. Jack was trouble and she knew it from the moment he walked into her classroom. He was a girl's dream. He was the real deal.

"That was so funny!" Ivy said.

"There's more to me that meets the eye."

Finch and Ivy entered the house, noisily, laughing about something that must have been a private joke between just the two of them. They could sense that something in the air had changed since they left.

"Okay, what did we miss?" Finch asked.

"Boy meets girl. Boy likes girl. Boy composes girl a lame song," Adam yelled.

Jack tossed another pillow at Adam.

Finch and Ivy laughed quietly.

CHAPTER 11

"You're just in time," Adam said. "Everyone ... take a look. The names of the members of Sector Twelve have been following Frank's movements for the past two years. Their names show up as bids for his research, same travel flights ... congressional visits ... your mother's funeral. They likely have someone on the inside at the agency ... ready to steal his designs. They are two steps ahead of us."

"That means ... we are being watched," Jack said.

"Agents are watching us and Sector Twelve is watching us, too. It's like sitting in a fishbowl," Finch said. "We'll just have to out-maneuver them."

"Let's not keep them waiting," Jack said. "There's a private road to the helicopter pad. It's not easy to find, so I'll take my car. The rest of you ride with Ivy; it's a short drive."

Jack watched the Range Rover in his rear view mirror. He was careful not to let the group fall too far behind. The path was a complex maze; you'd never know it was there unless you were looking for it. Frank traveled often, mostly on covert missions for the military. The private jet and helicopter was a necessary staple.

"A Bell 609," Sarah said, admiring the chopper. "I'm impressed; you don't see many of these in the private sector."

"A girl who knows her helicopters," he said, laughing.

"It's a civil twin-engine tilt rotor. I can fly this aircraft backwards, forwards, upside down and in circles," Sarah said.

"Forward would be nice," said Jack. "Let's keep this simple."

"Whatever you say."

"I have to say you constantly amaze me."

Sarah was quiet as they boarded the helicopter. She never thought of a proper response to Jack's comments. Mostly, she smiled and tried to remember to breathe. His compliment gave her chills and made her feel off-balance. *Don't let your guard down,* she thought. Jack was not going to make that easy and she knew it.

Onboard, Finch worked on the radar system. Ivy busied herself with the inventory supplies. Adam monitored the satellite and guidance system. Sarah and Jack took their positions in the pilot chairs. Jack began reading the helicopter's instruction manual, while Finch completed working with the control panel.

"You're kidding, right. I'm beginning to think you don't trust me," Sarah said, starting the engine.

"I just don't like surprises. I have to be ready to pilot if anything goes wrong. Besides, I can be a very useful co-pilot, if you'll let me help," Jack said, yelling over the noise of the propellers.

"I could drive, if the two of you can't make up your mind," Finch said, closing the control panel doors. I'm available to pilot, if there's a free chair."

"No!" Everyone shouted simultaneously from the passenger seats.

"I will try not to let your lack of confidence hurt my feelings," Finch laughed. "I tweaked the radar system so we're pretty much invisible. They won't see us coming. I'll be in my seat with the others if you change your mind."

"I've linked my computer to the pilot's controls," Adam shouted. "You should be able to see the transmissions onscreen. Follow the red blinking light – it should take us straight to Frank."

"Buckle your seats ladies and gentleman, we're off!" Sarah said.

The chopper lifted higher and higher off the ground until the houses were no longer visible. Amidst the chaos of taking off, no one noticed they were being watched. Two men sat obscurely in a dark-colored van, just outside of Jack's property. They quietly observed the helicopter on a high–powered telescope.

"You were right. They're on their way," one man said to the other. "We're headed back now."

Back on the helicopter, Jack and Sarah sat uncomfortably in the small space. They stared into the open sky, talking casually about the weather and school projects until Jack could no longer keep up the pretense.

"I don't want to waste time talking about things that don't matter," he said. "If this has taught me anything, it's that life is short. I want to know what you're feeling."

"I don't want to talk feelings Jack," she said. "Anyway, we have more pressing matters to discuss, don't you think?"

"Yes, but right now ... we're here ... together."

"Fine. What do you want to know?" Sarah asked.

"I am hoping that when this is over, you will allow me to take you on a date," Jack said.

"I don't think it would be appropriate, at least not while you're in my class. In fact, I don't think you should even think about something like that," she said.

"Aren't *you* ... thinking that?" Jack wanted to know.

Sarah was a hypocrite – she had been thinking that very thing. But for now, she wanted to be the responsible one. This could all go horribly wrong, and there was the added pressure of Frank's kidnapping to think about. She had to force herself back to reality – the alternative was too wild. *Stop the madness*, she told herself.

"I'm not in grade school. We're both over twenty one. Honestly, I'm having difficult time thinking about anything else while watching you fly this thing," Jack admitted. "It's very attractive... *You're* very attractive. "You don't know anything about me ... not really," Sarah said."

"Oh, but you are wrong about that. I do know about you," he said. "I told you before that I would never forget anything about you – I'm very observant."

"What have you observed?" Sarah asked quietly, nervously avoiding his eyes.

"Hmmm ... I know that you are very family oriented and that you miss your dad," Jack said.

59

"Anyone would know that," she smirked.

"I know you're beautiful, extremely smart and top-notch, dynamite pilot. You like reading romance novels by the fire; I saw the books at your house on the mantle. Let's see…you smile when you're nervous," he said, reaching to touch the corner of her cheek. "I know that you broke your pinkie finger when you were younger; it's still crooked. You listen to Justin Timberlake while jogging; you *only* jog early mornings at sunrise. You like to listen to Michael Buble in the shower and Avril Lavigne when you're sad … shall I continue?" Jack whispered.

"Please don't – it's too much information. I'm thinking of jumping," Finch yelled.

Finch was the only one that seemed bothered. Adam busied himself on the laptop, completely oblivious to everyone else and Ivy listened to Sonatas by Bach on her earphones.

"Wow, I'm just one big open book," Sarah smiled.

"Not to most people, I'd imagine," Jack said. "I'm just really interested, that's all. But we can change the subject for now, I can wait."

"How long before we get there?" Ivy yelled,

"Another thirty minutes or so," Sarah answered.

"Are you okay?" Finch asked Ivy. "You're not nervous, are you?"

"I'm fine. I was just thinking about school work – I know it sounds crazy, but it helps to focus on something I can actually control."

"The answer is yes, then. You are nervous," he said, ignoring her words; instead he listened to the tone of her voice.

"Why do you have to be such a know-it-all?" Ivy asked.

"It's just my way," he smiled, and so did she. "You're avoiding answering my question. Why are you nervous?"

"Well … let me see. It could be the fact that we're going a rescue mission against international kidnappers or maybe it's the fact that I'm in a helicopter eight thousand feet in the air, piloted by my Advanced Physics professor," Ivy reasoned. "I think my reaction is normal under the circumstances. The rest of you have me a little worried. You are all much too calm."

"We're going to be fine – I trust Jack," he said confidently. "Adam and I aren't too shabby either – these people won't know what hit them."

"You seem to have made an about face. You don't strike me as the kind of person who trusts easily," Ivy said.

"I don't. But I'm a good listener and I trust what I hear." Finch said. "Not much gets by my sensors."

Ivy was glad that Finch was so confident. His assurance made her feel better about things. She felt a twinge of guilt about not letting anyone know where she was, but she quickly ignored it. In hindsight, she would have made the same decision over again and she knew it. Her adoptive parents were generous and loving. They made sure she was exposed as much as possible to her Chinese heritage. They didn't visit as often as she'd like, which left Ivy ample time to devote to her education. Sometimes, the weight of being the perfect child seemed too great. She always felt the need to prove herself …to push past the crowd. She hated the word average.

"What's the plan once we get there?" Ivy yelled to Jack.

"We go in unnoticed. We find Frank. We get out of Dodge, fast," he shouted in response.

Sarah stared blankly at Jack.

"What are you looking at?" He asked.

She was silent.

"What are you thinking? Say it," he pressed when she didn't answer.

"That's the plan?" She asked, stammering over the words and looking at him incredulously.

"Yep. That's the plan," Jack said.

"I'd really feel better if you had a plan B," Sarah said.

CHAPTER 12

Back in Texas, Frank slowly regained consciousness. He waited while his eyes adjusted to the light and he focused on his surroundings. He was seated in the center of a room, with his hands tied behind his back. He was acutely aware of his hands cramping and he tried to wiggle them to get the circulation flowing. He struggled against the ropes, but they wouldn't give.

"Think, Frank ... think," he said softly. "How did I get here?"

He concentrated on remembering. He searched through the images in his brain as he tried to make sense of everything. Slowly, the pieces of the puzzle connected. Suddenly, he could remember everything clearly. He remembered the meeting at the coffee shop with Lincoln and the men in black suits. He remembered, too, being shot with the dart gun. The memory made him think about the pain – his neck stiffened.

Frank looked around; he was not alone. Three very large men in military fatigues positioned themselves around the room. Two men stood at the door with guns and one man sat stone-faced at a computer desk near the wall. There was a small window above where the man sat and he noticed the sun was going down.

"How long have I been here," he asked himself.

"Could I talk to whoever is in charge?" Frank asked. His voice was raspy and hoarse.

The men ignored him completely. They said nothing to acknowledge his presence. They did not even look in his direction.

"Is there someone I can talk to? Why am I here?" Frank decided to try again, but it was no use, these men were not prepared to talk. Frank sat for hours in silence.

He surveyed the room for tools, taking mental inventory of any item that he could later use to help him escape. He planned for an escape, focusing all of his energy on getting home to Jack.

"I'm certain that you know who I am. Surely, someone has informed you that I'm a wealthy man of almost limitless means. I will give you any amount you ask … if you will let me go, right now."

The men said nothing again. The room was perfectly still. There was unquestionable silence, except this time, they glared at Frank, menacingly.

"I guess asking to go to the bathroom is out of the question, then?" he joked.

"There is one door that leads in and out of the room. There are two windows, but it is undetermined what floor I'm on. The three men are armed," Frank reported to himself.

"Who's in charge here?" There was still no response.

Frank had an advantage. He built obscure, unassuming gadgets that were inconspicuous to most onlookers. Inside his watch was a tiny, microscopic transmitter, which he used to send coded messages to Jack. It was a challenge to manipulate the buttons because of the handcuffs, but he managed to work around the tight shackles.

"Could I speak to whoever gives the orders?" Frank asked for the third time.

One of the men walked over to him.

"Yes, we know who you are. You don't get to ask the questions, Mr. Prince. We're told to keep you alive, for now, but I may easily forget those orders if you continue with your silly requests," the man said, striking him in the face with the back of the pistol.

"It was a simple question!" Frank shouted.

"I've told you already," the man growled, punching him in the stomach. "Keep quiet if you know what's good for you. No more questions!"

"I'll rephrase, tell whoever is in charge that I would like to talk – that's not a question," Frank said, tasting the subtle hint of blood in his mouth.

The man turned and walked out the door, stopping to whisper something to the two guards. Frank started to whistle, hoping the noise would cover up the beeping on his watch. He tried to send more messages, this time using Morse code to Jack's cell phone.

"Seriously guys – is there a restroom in this place?" Neither of the two men moved nor said anything.

"I should have hidden a key on my wristband," Frank whispered. "A universal key would have been a good thing to have. I've got to remember that when I get home."

The guards opened the door. The sound of footsteps approaching echoed in the air. The man dressed in military fatigues returned. Lincoln, from the coffee shop, followed close behind.

"How are you Frank?" Lincoln asked.

He leaned over and looked into Frank's eyes.

"You are shorter than I remember," Frank mocked. "You don't look intimidating at all. You should let me go before someone gets hurt."

"I'm trying to be polite. You do not need to hurl insults at me. It will not help your cause, Mr. Prince. I've asked you a question, but you have not answered me. How are you?"

"I've been better – what am I doing here?" Frank asked with disgust.

"You are here because your country needs you," Lincoln said. "If you cooperate, you will be a hero."

"You do not represent my country – what do you want?"

"Money, power, and world domination," he said. "Of course, I want your energy formula, as well."

"Wow, is *that* all?" Frank asked, grimacing. He shifted uncomfortably in his chair. "You will most certainly bring destruction and chaos down around you, if you allow the formula to get into the wrong hands. This is a mistake. Innocent people will get hurt. What do you expect me to say? I will not agree to whatever it is that has made you bring me here."

"We want you to build a weapon," Lincoln continued. "You have a formula for a battery cell. A battery that generates its own power … that never needs recharging. It's remarkable, really. You have caught our attention. We want the formula before anyone else gets it. You are in such demand. We are not the kind of people who stand in lines, as you can imagine. It is simple – you will give it to us."

"How do you even know about the battery – it's confidential."

"We are everywhere," Lincoln stated arrogantly.

"We ...," Frank repeated. "You are part of Sector 12."

"Bingo. See, I knew you were a smart man, that's why we need your help." Lincoln said, pacing back and forth like a lion about to pounce.

"You seem much too on edge for a man in charge," Frank said. "Someone has, no doubt given you instructions for me. What has been said? What command has been given for my captivity?"

"Your confidence may backfire on you. I warn you to cooperate or suffer the consequences."

"I'm not going to help you do anything. You should let me go before this gets out of hand. We are both men in power, used to getting what we want. You must know that I will not easily give you what you want," Frank said. "My designs are to make the environment safe. I will not see them reduced to weapons used by terrorists. Power should be used for good."

"Good is subjective," Lincoln said.

"Let me go and I will consider what you have asked."

"You're not going anywhere...unless I say so," he said leaning over next to Frank's ear. "You will help me … or maybe we should wait until Jack arrives. Maybe then, you will be more cooperative. I, too, am a family man. I hate the thought of having to put your son in harm's way but well, what choice will you leave me, unless you volunteer to cooperate? You will force me to do something I do not wish to do, Frank. I will do it, however, if I am pushed too far."

"If you touch my son – I will make sure that you live to regret it." The veins on Frank's head bulged and he hissed between tightly clamped teeth. "Don't you dare threaten my family, Lincoln. Don't test me on this point. If your bosses know anything about me, they will surely know that I can be a very formidable enemy and I like to win. That is what you have gained today … an enemy, with a very long memory. You will not be able to hide – the earth will not be a big enough place to hide you from me when this is over."

"Look around you Frank. I've got you already. Look at yourself, the almighty Frank Prince, secret agent and multibillionaire. The genius software developer with the golden touch and you're in *my* house!" Lincoln said, coldly. "You will do what we say or your family — what's left of it, will die. You're not going anywhere...unless we say so. You should really try and be nicer to me, Frank – if you know what's good for you."

"You're acting as if you are in charge, but we both know that you are not smart enough to set this up yourself, Lincoln. I want to talk to your boss. Go and tell your boss that I have an offer to discuss with him. Tell him that if he wants me to cooperate, then he must come here and face me."

"You get to talk to me only, Frank. If you want something – you talk to me," Lincoln snarled. "As far as you're concerned, I'm all you've got," he maniacally scoffed. He was fuming. "You are much too arrogant for your own good. It will be nice to teach you a lesson."

"As you said, you have me – I'm here. It seems we are at an impasse," Frank said. "What happens now?"

Two of the men moved closer, with their weapons drawn. Lincoln motioned for them to remain in position. They returned to their post at the door, but they did not relax. The guards continued to keep eye contact with their guns pointed to Frank. The room was noticeably tense.

"Frank, I am not posturing," Lincoln said. "I am doing this for the money. It's business. I will do whatever is necessary to get what I want."

"So, you kidnapped me and brought me to God knows where … for money?"

"You're in Texas – where I am meeting buyers who are interested in the formula as fuel and I told them I knew where I could get it. You are going to give me the formula or you are going to be very sorry."

"You had to know I wouldn't do it, no matter what you said," Frank shouted. "You already knew that I would not volunteer anything, regardless of your threats."

"I did," Lincoln admitted. "But I knew you could be persuaded. We have been following you for some time, Frank and well....I think you will come around to our way of thinking. You are not as complex as you may think. But you are probably too caught up in your own self–importance to know it. We will see what it takes to bend your will."

Frank's thoughts went to Jack. It made him uneasy hearing Lincoln discuss his son with such callous disregard. The plan was to stall as long as he could. If necessary he would have Lincoln believe he'd join them. In reality, he prayed for a way out before Jack arrived.

"Let's wait for Jack and see what happens, shall we?" Lincoln continued his ranting. "Maybe Jack will motivate you to cooperate."

"How does Sector 12 fit into all this?" Frank asked, changing the subject.

"Sector 12 … well, we would prefer anonymity. You need not concern yourself with such things. You will not be around to be of any consequence to us. But, if you consent to team with us, I can make your remaining days comfortable. We are not so bad once you get to know us."

"I cannot agree to your terms. It does not matter how you rephrase your request. I will never agree," Frank said. "I know that if I give you what you want – you will kill me. And if I refuse to give you what you want – well, you will kill me still. I cannot see how I can win with those two alternatives."

"Yes, we have a dilemma, don't we? How unfortunate it is that we could not agree, but since we have reached a dead end, there is really nothing more to discuss," Lincoln said. "We have talked enough for now. Nothing need be done yet. Things change quickly. You will see."

Lincoln left with one of the guards. The remaining two men stood at the door.

"I hope you got my messages," Frank whispered to himself. It was almost a prayer. He was confident in his son's ability to decipher the clues. He questioned his decision, however, to send the messages in the first place.

THE POWER

CHAPTER 13

Sarah landed the helicopter in an open field near the coordinate point.

"It's just like riding a bike," she said. "I forgot how much I loved flying. I'm going to have to make this part of my recreational activities when we return."

"It's quiet," Jack said.

"This is outside the military's knowledge. So, they would want to keep out of sight and not have too many guards outside, but don't underestimate their weapons – they're armed and they will shoot first and ask second."

"We will have to be smarter and faster, then," Jack said.

"You make it sound so easy," Adam said. "Somehow I don't think they are going to let us walk in and out without incident."

"No, I don't mean to imply that it will be a walk in the park, but I am certain that we will prevail," Jack replied.

"Let's talk logistics. This plant has three floors," Sarah said. "The location that we are looking for is underground. We will need to disable the cameras and get past two electronic doors with a key pass. If you can get one off of one of the guards, then great, otherwise you will need to disable the key pad which may be more difficult."

"What is the procedure once we find where they're keeping Frank?" Ivy asked.

"If you find the room where they're keeping my dad – don't go in alone; wait for the rest of us. The laser gun will paralyze the guards, but I'm not sure for how long. Keep your radio frequency open in case there is trouble."

Sarah took the lead. They ran across the field and landed at the side entrance of the building, trying to avoid the rotating cameras. Jack and the others waited for the cameras to move before kneeling outside the plant door.

"There's a guard, just inside the door," Sarah said. "We should draw him out."

"Maybe I should stay on the plane and wait for you guys to come out," Adam said. "I could keep watch out here and monitor the radios."

"You are such a girl," Ivy said. "I think it's safer if you stay with the group. You could trip over your own shadow if we leave you by yourself."

"Shh, someone is coming – heads up," Finch warned.

The guard stepped outside the door and Jack shot him with his laser gun. The guard dropped to the floor convulsing before becoming completely stiff. Adam and Ivy moved his motionless body out of sight before anyone from inside the building noticed.

"That's not so bad for a tinker toy. I told you it would work," Jack said smugly.

Sarah and Jack headed left toward the stairwell. Adam, Finch and Ivy were already heading around the corner, maneuvering undetected past guards at a desk.

"We need to get out of sight," Finch said. The elevator is going to open in any minute now."

They ducked inside an empty room. Adam looked around the room, while Finch and Ivy guarded the door.

"What is all this?" he asked.

"What do you see?" Finch asked.

"This computer shows transactions going to Swiss bank accounts. It looks like Sector Twelve is nothing more than money hungry terrorist that will buy and sell anything, from classified government secrets, to selling weapons to the highest bidder. They are lowly opportunists."

"They want Frank's designs to sell them," Ivy said.

"Incoming," Finch said. "A guard is coming. He's on the right."

Ivy was ducked low to the ground on the right side of the room near where the guard was entering. The guard very slowly entered the room looking around for movement. Ivy kicked the gun out of his hand and then ducked, barely missing a blow from his fist. She spun around and kicked him off balance and then Finch immobilized him with the laser gun.

"Is everyone ok?" Finch asked.

"We're alive, if that's what you mean," she said. "We're in better shape than the guard, who apparently won't be able to move for a couple of hours."

"That was too close guys," Adam said, downloading the data from the computer. There are names, dates, accounts … everything we need to track down all the people involved."

"This is kind of exciting, don't you think?" Ivy asked.

"Is this your idea of adventure? If so, a guy might find it difficult to measure up," Finch smiled.

"What can I say, I'm not your average girl," she replied. "I admit this is a neurotic type of fun, for anyone. I know I should be scared out of my wits, but that makes it more adventurous. I will, in all likelihood, need to see a therapist one day."

Sarah and Jack exited the stairwell and headed toward black double doors at the end of the hall. They halted when they heard voices approaching from inside the doors. They quickly searched for an unlocked door in the hallway. They finally found a small storage room unlocked and hurried inside and waited. They could see a shadow moving from underneath the door. Sarah inhaled when the door handle jiggled. Jack put his hand over her mouth. He pointed to a narrow vent in the ceiling.

"We can hide there," he whispered.

Jack climbed up first and helped Sarah, leaping quickly upon the top of cardboard boxes and into the narrow opening that was barely wide enough for the both of them.

"Great," she breathed. "Did you plan this?"

"I'm not this creative," he said.

She stood in front of him face to face in the very small tunnel, tightly pressed against him. Jack's arm was curved around her back for support and she could feel the warmth of him making the small space seem even smaller. He was taller than she. Her face was inches from his neck. If she moved forward an inch, her mouth would touch the hollow of his throat and she tried to remain still. It was quiet. For a while, they could only hear each other breathing until the men entered the storage room below.

Three men stood below them gathering items from the storage space and packing them into bags. Jack and Sarah were forced to keep still and wait until the men finished. But the closeness of their positions made it unbearably difficult to concentrate on anything except each other. Jack leaned in to ask Sarah if she was okay. He paused to inhale the scent of her and his cheek rubbed against her neck and his arm tightened unconsciously. Jack closed his eyes and imagined them somewhere else, somewhere alone and not in danger.

Sarah was glad that she could not see his face. She was acutely aware of Jack, his scent, his chest against her and his arm on her back which seemed to burn her skin.

"I can't breathe," she exhaled.

Jack loosened his arm. But that's not what Sarah wanted to happen.

"I think I'm claustrophobic," she said.

When she leaned backward, her laser gun slipped and nearly fell to the floor. Jack was quick and caught it before it hit the floor. Then men below were still unaware of their presence.

Sarah stood back up, trying to put distance between her and Jack, but there was no room. She tilted her head up to whisper something, but her mind went blank.

"That was close," Sarah whispered.

"Anytime," he said, sending light puffs of air over her face.

Sarah had a strong urge to turn her face slightly so that her lips touched his. Her head was against his chest and wanted to move but something seemed to hold her there. Neither of them noticed that the men had finished packing the boxes and were already leaving. It was only when the door slammed shut that Jack and Sarah came back to reality. They stood motionless for a few moments longer.

CHAPTER 14

"I think we can climb down now," Sarah said.

"What did you say?" Jack asked, staring at her.

"The men have left. It's safe," she said.

Sarah and Jack climbed down cautiously and jumped to the floor.

"What were they doing in here anyway?" Sarah asked.

They were packing C-4," Jack said, inspecting the contents of the boxes. "There's enough material in this room to blow up a small city. Let's get out of here. I think they're keeping my dad in the room with the double doors. It's the only one under lock and key."

"I agree," Sarah said. "You'll need to disable the key pad before someone   notices   us."

"I'm going to need a few minutes … keep an eye out," Jack said, using his tools to remove the key pad cover and disable the lock.

"Hurry," Sarah said.

"It's done. The lock is disabled. Be careful," Jack said, opening the door.

Inside the room, a dark shadow hit him on the head. He dropped to his knees but quickly regained his composure. Sarah took aim and shot the man, paralyzing him.

"Nice shot. Thanks," Jack said, getting to his feet.

"Watch out," Frank shouted from the center of the room.

Two of the guards ran toward Jack. He picked up two large sticks from a shelf and banged them against one guard's head, turned and hit a final blow to the second guard's chest the other one lay collapsed.

"You broke his ribcage. I heard them crack," Sarah said with excitement.

"Yes, but he will live," Jack answered.

"Wow, Jack that was impressive. Where'd you learn that?"

"Ninja turtles," he said.

"You're kidding, really?" she asked.

"What?" he asked. ..."Anthropomorphic turtles, trained in the art of ninjutsu – they're named after Renaissance artists. "Well, it worked, didn't it?" Jack asked, laughing. "Duck!" Jack yelled. "Look behind you!"

One of the guards had come up from behind and lunged at Sarah. But she was quick – she ducked and punched, then pounded him again with her backpack. She kneed him and elbowed him to the face and he fell, bleeding from his eyes and nose.

"Where'd that move come from?" Jack asked.

"Blind dates from hell," she said. "It works every time."

"Dad, are you all right?"

"Ask me later; let's get out of here first, if you don't mind," Frank responded.

"Do I know you?" Frank looked at Sarah.

"Sarah, this is my dad, Frank Prince. Dad, meet Professor Sarah London," Jack introduced them awkwardly.

"You're his professor from school?" He asked, bewildered. "This is a long way to come for an assignment, isn't it?"

"Let's save the small talk for later," Jack said hurriedly. "We should go," he added, patting Frank on the back.

Frank looked at his son and winked, gesturing his approval of Sarah. He couldn't stop smiling at the two of them. Jack laughed at his dad's gesture because he and his dad had found it difficult in the past to communicate on any level; yet now, they seemed to read each other's minds. Jack was pleased that Frank approved of his friendship with Sarah, as if he didn't have anything else to think about, like trying to get as far away from this place as possible.

Lincoln had other plans. He entered the door with three men following on either side, just as Frank was untied from the chair.

"Well, well, well, isn't this a nice reunion and just so...expected. I saw you coming, Jack. You are here because I allowed you to be. I thought your presence might motivate Frank to give me what I want. I'm sorry Frank, but I took a lot of effort to get you here and I cannot just let you walk out the door," Lincoln said.

As if on cue, the men pointed guns to their heads and took their backpack and laser guns then tied the three of them to chairs.

"What do you hope to get from all this?" Jack asked.

"Isn't it obvious...world peace," Lincoln mocked. "The people will surely rejoice with us as we rule. Peace is attainable, Jack – at a cost, of course. And no doubt, we shall profit from it. That is our utopia – the plan has been laid."

"How shall you achieve peace by selling weapons to the highest bidder?"

"Well, there is that, of course. Specifically one hundred seventy five million dollars and all I need is the formula for the battery. But, for the record, I am not selling weapons, just a battery ... a source of fuel. I am not responsible for what some nefarious person may or may not decide to do," Lincoln scoffed.

"You're a charlatan – a pretender and a fraud," Frank shouted. "You are just a hired gun and can no more deliver what you promise than I can make it rain. You and the people you work for are nothing more than thieves and opportunists who prey on society, with your twisted version of the truth. I am sure that telling yourself you're not responsible for the actions of others helps you sleep at night, when in fact – it is a lie."

"Maybe you're right," Lincoln confessed. "Maybe what you say is true – I will not deny it. But you miss the beauty of the plan and that is this: I will be long gone to a place where no one can find me by the time anyone figures out my connection. I have had years to think about this and to prepare for every scenario."

"Well, Frank, what's it going to be? You have had time to weigh your options. I am not a patient man," Lincoln said, putting the gun to Jack's head and twisting his hand forward to add pressure.

"I will give you the code," Frank said, surrendering only to buy them more time to think of a plan to escape. "The code is much too complicated and convoluted to figure out unless you know what you're looking for. I will help you decipher it and build the battery for you."

"It's now or never Frank," Lincoln said. He stood in front of the computer, tapping his foot impatiently and glaring. What is the password code?"

"The code is BigDaddy1999," Frank whispered so low that no one heard him.

"I didn't hear you Frank. Stop mumbling and give me the code," he said shouting.

"The code is b–i–g–d–a–d–d–y–1–9–9–9," he said slowly and clearly, spelling the words. "Really, dad?" Jack grinned, shaking his head.

Sarah put her head down and blushed a little between laughter.

"What?" Frank asked aloud, as if he didn't know what everyone was talking about.

The password opened the file and a list of symbols scrolled down the screen.

"Perfect. It's perfect," Lincoln said, almost chanting. He concentrated all of his attention onto the formula, staring blankly – as if a trance. He tapped his hand on the desk repeatedly while writing notes on a piece of paper. Soon the trance was broken and Lincoln shifted to Frank.

"You have exactly twenty-four hours to make me a workable prototype that I can show my buyers. I will get you all the supplies you need. Once I have a demonstration that it works, you can all go home. Be good Frank and this will be over in twenty-four hours. If you give me any trouble, I will kill all of you. It seems like an easy choice to make," Lincoln threatened.

He turned on his heels and walked away, leaving the armed guards in place at the door. The room looked suddenly darker and ominous now that he was gone. The threats hung in the air like a heavy cloud before a storm. Frank and Jack exchanged looks and spoke to each other in hushed tones that only they could hear.

Frank inhaled and exhaled deeply, closing his eyes.

"Tell me that you have a plan B?" he asked Jack, trying to make his movements as slight as possible, so the guards wouldn't notice. Sarah looked at Jack to show her agreement with Frank's statement. She fought the urge to say *I told you so,* but the words were on the tip of her tongue, ready to spill out in any moment. She smiled to herself automatically, taking a minute to assess this new relationship. She thought Jack looked a lot like Frank – maybe not so much physically, but their behavior and mannerisms seemed similar. Frank was definitely more refined and polished. That was encouraging. It gave her a small window into the future. She was hopeful that Jack would develop the same finesse. She was certain that he would mature as gracefully as his father.

*

Adam, Ivy and Finch hid in an empty room to avoid lurking guards. Finch's hearing was pretty good, so they were able to prevent bumping into the guards by hiding before they saw them. "More guards are coming," Finch said. "Hide!"

They quickly scattered as the footsteps got closer. They kneeled down behind a couple of desks in the vacant room. Finch listened as the men spoke in the hallway. He could hear one man call the other, "Lincoln." The rest of the words were in a foreign language.

"It's Russian," Ivy said quietly. The man named Lincoln said, "Let's give Mr. Prince the supplies he needs for the battery. We need him to build the battery – that's the most important thing now. Once we have it, take care of them, including the young boy and the girl. We can't have any loose ends. Is that clear?"

"What else are they saying?" Finch asked.

"Lincoln told them to keep a tight watch on them so there was no mix up," Ivy translated.

"Jack, can you hear me?" Adam spoke into the radio. There was no response and he tried again. "Jack is not answering. We had better find them – something's wrong."

"Let's keep moving then," Adam said.

Finch bumped into one of the desks as he stood and knocked over some books onto the floor. The noise got the attention of the guards outside the door and Finch backed away from the door. He crouched down low to listen. They were coming into the room and approaching fast. Finch leaned his head to one side, looking at

Adam and Ivy; he waved them back behind the table. He heard the door creak open and the footsteps were now inside the room moving cautiously toward him – and another set of footsteps followed close behind. Finch braced himself for the assault. His fists tightened, squeezing his palms, until they hurt.

Adam saw the guard's shadow get closer and closer.

"He's on your right," he told Finch.

"I hear him," Finch nodded.

The man leaned over the desk to see where the noise was coming from. Finch stood quickly and elbowed him, breaking his nose and struck a final blow to the man's head which knocked him out. There was a second guard stopped near Ivy, looking over the desk where she was hidden.

She took the offensive, running leap toward her attacker and kicked him with such a force that knocked him off balance to his knees. The man slowly regained equilibrium and stood again and moved toward Ivy with his fist raised. She jumped over the top of his head and reached her arms up backward and grabbed the man by the neck and flipped him forward, leaving him pinned to the ground. Ivy reached in her pouch, while still keeping the man pinned and stabbed him in the neck with the dart. She stood and placed her foot on the man's chest – she enjoyed herself more than she should have. Ivy thought to herself that the practice would keep her on her toes. She thought that if she looked at it this way – it would not seem so fool hearty to go off with her friends.

"Enough fun, guys – let's find Jack," Adam said.

They left the room and barricaded the door behind them. Adam found a control room and peeked in to see security guards watching camera monitors. He reached in the backpack and pulled out three circular gold marbles and rolled them underneath the door into the room where the guards sat. The marbles released a clear, non–toxic gas. The men could be heard coughing from inside. Adam waited until he heard an audible thud as the men fell unconsciousness. Then, only silence was heard and that's when Adam opened the door and went inside the room.

"Think of it as a sleeping pill," Adam said to Ivy. "They'll be out for a couple of hours, but they will be fine."

Adam used the security cameras to search all the rooms in the building to locate Jack. Finally, he breathed, "I found them – they're tied up in a room downstairs with black double doors. Let's go."

Ivy watched the hallway as Adam and Finch worked on the controls. Before leaving, Adam took a screwdriver and wedged it into the wiring system to shut down the cameras.

"Let's go – the room that we want is down the hall and to the right to the third door at the end of the hallway," he said.

They found the room with the black double doors. They burst in with the element of surprise. "Three o'clock high," Adam yelled to his friend. "He's a tall one."

Finch slid on his knees, grabbing the guard's gun, standing and swinging the gun around to a loud blow to the back of the man's head.

Ivy was preoccupied defending herself against another guard. She propelled against the wall and kicked the guard with all her might sending him flying head first to the floor.

"Let's move out fast guys," Adam said. "There are more guards coming."

Another two guards ran into the room but Finch and Ivy kicked the guns from their hands. Both of them fought off the guards with synchronized precision, moving back and forth in each other's path taking turns with rhythmic punches that left the men crumpled on the floor.

"You could hear their movements," she said, making her words almost sound like a question.

"The ears don't lie," Finch confirmed. "I see the sound vibrations as images – it's difficult to explain really. It may help to think of it this way: every sound has its own image. Since all matter is energy, any movement – even the slightest of movements are turned into images in my mind. It makes responding to it almost natural."

"I think I understand. I have more questions, but that will have to do for now, I suppose. Thank you," she said. We Have A Problem.

Back in the control room, men in camouflage fatigues kicked the door down and discovered the unconscious guards on the floor.

The men attempted to sound an alarm – but it no longer worked, thanks to Adam, who had earlier disabled the security system, which included the door locks and the alarm system.

"We have a problem down here in the control room," the man spoke into the radio.

"I do not like to be disturbed. My sole focus is getting the batter made and ready for the overseas buyers. This had better be important," Lincoln said.

"The system is offline," the man said.

"Then fix it!" Lincoln yelled into the phone and disconnected the call.

"The B Team has arrived," Adam said entering the room with the black double doors. "They can't lock us out now that all the controls have been shut down. They must hate that!"

Finch and Ivy followed close behind, moving methodically in concert. They had an undeniable rhythm as if they were playing a duet together. Finch would move and Ivy would fill the gaps in between. When Ivy moved, Finch reacted with a similar pattern as if there was some prior collaboration. It was a harmony of sorts.

Two very large armed guards were monitoring the room. When Adam entered, the guards ran toward the team. Ivy and Finch fired lasers in the direction of the guards. Finch got an early hit and the guard fell to the floor. Ivy ran toward the second guard. She jumped onto the man lying on the ground and used his body like a trampoline, to catapult into the air, landing on the second. She brought him down with the slightest pressure to the back of his neck, rendering him unconscious.

"Take that!" Ivy boasted aloud, smiling at her accomplishment.

"You are too good to be true," Finch said, giving her a high five. "But I had him. I could have taken him. You know that, right?"

"Of course. Whatever you say," Ivy smiled.

"We're over here, guy!" Jack yelled, as Adam untied him. "What took you so long?"

"They didn't exactly roll out the red carpet for us – but we're here, now. You are welcome," Ivy said sarcastically.

"Thank you," Jack said, as he loosened the ropes and wiggled out of them. He grabbed the duffel bag that had been tossed aside by the guard and handed it over to Adam.

"Here ... you know what to do. I will untie Sarah and Frank and meet you at the chopper – get out as fast as you can," Jack told them. "Go now!"

Adam, Ivy and Finch left with a quick glance back, before running down the hall.

Jack began untying Frank's rope when he felt a blow to the back of his head. He reached up to touch the bump that was forming, and then fell limply the floor, barely conscious – his eyes rolled back and forth. He could barely focus. He was vaguely aware of Lincoln and two security guards standing over him as he lay motionless on the floor. He was trying to will his body to move but nothing was happening. He looked at his hand, trying desperately to move it. He could almost hear his brain sending a message to his body to get up.

"See what you made me do, Frank," Lincoln said, in a menacing tone. "I'm usually a very reasonable person. I don't like to resort to violence. It's so... savage and barbaric. Do you want to be the cause of your son's death? Is that it – because that is most definitely the road you are traveling with all these heroics? I tried to be patient – but my resolve is wearing thin. Maybe, just maybe, I overestimated your love for your son. You have put him at grave risk."

"Leave him alone, Lincoln," Frank shouted. "This is between you and me. Leave these kids out of this and we can talk, man to man," he said. "You will never get me to cooperate if you hurt my son. I will have no motivation to give you what you want if you harm him, do you understand?" Frank pleaded. "Let's not end things this way. We can still talk, you and me – alone."

"No.... I think we are way past talking," Lincoln said, standing over Jack, glaring at him with satisfaction. "This must be very hard for you, having just lost Mary last year. It was such a shame how she died, so tragically," he said. "Mary was a good agent and usually so very careful – it was a shame," Lincoln whispered and shook his head, with a devious glint in his eyes as if there were hidden meaning in his words.

"Tell me, Frank. It was the same day that you decided to scrap the plans to move forward with the battery, wasn't it?" he pushed for information. "Mary had gathered the plans and was leaving the building. Someone must have been following her and ran her car off the road," he said. "It's a shame they attacked her ... and just left her there in the street ... to die. It must have been unbearable for you, Frank."

"How do you know so much about my wife's death?"

"Life can be cruel, don't you think?" Lincoln asked, ignoring Frank's question. "The attackers took your designs and her purse and jewelry to make everyone think it was a routine robbery."

"That information was never made public," Frank said. "How do you know what happened?"

"You should not have been so selfish with your work. Obviously, there are people very interested in carrying the project further. These people will do anything, apparently," Lincoln said.

"Did you have anything to do with Mary's death?" Frank asked.

"Me ... no ... no, of course not," Lincoln said. "But people like me, unfortunately did not care that Mary was in their way. They were heartless, I agree."

"Did Sector Twelve have anything to do with it? Were they after my designs that day?" Frank yelled.

"I cannot say. The only reason I bring it up is to say don't repeat the mistake. Are you prepared to risk Jack's life by refusing to cooperate?" Lincoln asked. "It doesn't have to be this way, Frank. But, of course, the decision is yours alone. You could build the battery and go back to your boring, pathetic lives," Lincoln said. "What is it going to be? For all of your noble words on morality, character and American values ... *this* is the question that stumps you?"

"You wouldn't understand anything of life and value," Frank said. "That conversation would be over your head. You cannot comprehend the concept of true humanity. It's not in your nature. I wouldn't waste my time – you would never understand."

Jack's hand twitched as he lay on the floor. Out of the corner of his eye, he saw something move. Whenever his hand shifted left, he saw the laser gun on the table shift to the left. Sarah observed the movement, too. She gasped.

"It's kinetic energy," she said, whispering in a barely audible breath of confusion and awe.

Jack focused completely on willing the gun to move to his hand and it did. He felt energy flow through his body. He felt his brain communicating with his hands and feet ... he felt everything. Jack aimed the gun at the guard and he fell to the floor in a convulsing lump. Everything happened so fast. Every mathematical formula and scientific equation came to life in one split second.

Jack dropped the gun and put his hands out toward the guard and swayed to the left, sending the man flying into the wall. Jack swayed his hands to the right and the other guard flew into the wall on the right side of the room.

"Did I just see that? Did that really happen?" Sarah asked as Jack untied them.

"I knew it!" Frank said to himself. "That was amazing, son. I've always known you were capable of such power."

"What's happening?" Lincoln asked, backing away. "How is that possible?"

Jack pushed both hands out and objects floated in the air in a whirlwind. Boxes lifted to the ceiling, and the contents spilled over onto the floor. The tables flew across the room, breaking into pieces as they crashed onto the wall. Lincoln's body was lifted off the floor and he hovered for a few minutes, before he floated against the wall and was unable to move.

"Put me down," Lincoln fumed. "I insist that you put me down now!"

"If you insist," Jack said, lowering his hands, letting him fall to the floor.

"Matter and energy are really different but the same. It's tapping into brainpower! It's about letting the right side in on what the left side is thinking. Einstein's theory of relativity, algorithms, Isaac Newton's law of gravity all work with same premise," Jack explained while moving objects through the air. "If you could write a program that could connect the dots of the brain and access every piece of information at one time...understanding creation itself...understanding energy...," his voice trailed off.

"Power," Sarah and Frank said in unison. They stared wide–eyed at Jack as if he had just discovered fire. No one knew what to say. For several minutes, everyone was silent. They were all stunned until the ceiling started to fall down around them. Explosive, thunderous sounds came from outside.

The explosions continued; they could be heard throughout the building. Plaster fell from the ceiling and tremors shook the foundation beneath them. Sarah and Frank jumped as they felt the floor rumble.

"What's happening out there," they asked. "It felt like an earthquake. What is that noise?"

"I believe that is Adam's way of telling us that it's time to go," Jack laughed, flashing his beautiful white teeth. He grabbed Sarah's hand and motioned for Frank to make a quick exit. "The helicopter is waiting. We should hurry," Jack said, running out the door. "Adam is probably wondering what's taking us so long."

"You don't have to tell me twice. I'm ready," Sarah said. "Let's go home."

The halls were filled with noise from the explosion and the smell of burnt ashes. Jack was feeling much more confident and stronger even. He blew open doors with the wave of his hand. His mind was working in perfect harmony with all of his faculties. He felt completely aware and in perfect balance for the first time in a long time. Purpose and power united, giving him a renewed sense of courage. A surge of energy pulsed throughout Jack's body. He had never felt so alive.

Frank reached the exit doors first. It was dark outside now and their eyes adjusted to the night. They kept running toward the direction of the helicopter. Jack didn't immediately notice at first that he was running much faster than the others and they had fallen behind.

One of the guards grabbed Sarah from behind. She could not see the man's face as she tried to keep him from choking her.

"Let me go! You don't know what you're doing. You'll regret this!" Sarah yelled, gasping for air. "Somebody help me!"

Jack turned to find that Sarah was no longer behind him. He retraced his steps through the dark, smoke-filled night. He saw the guard holding Sarah. The man had a gun to her head and had his other arm around her neck. Jack could hear the gun click and Sarah squinted her eyes shut, anticipating the next move. Jack moved quickly, stretching his arms toward the guard, forcing him to release Sarah. Frank immediately ran to her and pulled her forward. They ran as fast as they could to the helicopter, leaving Jack to take care of the guards.

"Get as far away as you can, right now," Jack yelled to them. "Things are about to get a little messy."

"What about you?" Frank yelled back.

"I'll be right behind you, I promise," Jack said. "Trust me dad, I've got things under control. Don't worry."

Jack shoved his hands forward with such force that it lifted the guard off the ground and sent him flying backward into the burning building.

"Get on the chopper, now!" Jack yelled to the others.

The guards were still advancing toward them and shooting guns toward the chopper. Jack lifted a nearby vehicle off the ground with the wave of his hand and sent it sliding across the field trapping the men. He then caused a huge dust cloud to form by circling his arms. The dust cloud shielded Jack and his friends as they boarded the chopper.

"Dude, you have got to show me how to do that!" Adam yelled in amazement. He had been watching everything from the door of the helicopter. "Now that's the way to make an exit! That was the single, most exciting thing I've ever seen," he continued to ramble on about explosions and flying cars.

"Would someone sit him down, please?" Ivy pleaded.

"Take that! That's the way we do it," Adam exclaimed.

"Get in the helicopter, Adam, and sit down before you hurt yourself," Jack said. "Is everyone present and accounted for?"

"We're all here and ready to take off," Sarah shouted from the pilot's seat.

"What is going on?" Finch asked. "I have never heard vibrations of that magnitude. What happened out there?"

"You won't believe it!" Sarah yelled from the pilot's seat. "*I* don't even believe it."

"Somebody tell me," Finch said, looking around.

Frank sat in the co-pilot's chair beside Sarah. "That was something back there, wasn't it?"

"Explosive," she said, smiling. "I just didn't think it was my business to talk about what happened. If Jack wants to explain it – he can ... when he's ready."

"I completely understand. It's mind-blowing. It's a lot to process," Frank said, buckling his seatbelt.

"So, what really happened out there, Adam?" Finch whispered.

"Jack is the man, that's what happened," he shouted. "You should have seen it! No offense, man."

"None taken," Finch said. "Keep talking ... what happened?"

"I'm not sure how to explain it. It was like Jack was struck with a lightning bolt or something and all of sudden, he was moving things with his hands, lifting cars off the ground, hurling people through walls. That's pretty much it."

"No one went through a wall," Ivy corrected.

"Don't interrupt my story," Adam said.

"I get the idea," Finch said quietly. "I would have liked to have seen that as well. I know it's possible...I mean anything is possible, right? I've studied the equations in books and researched similar theories on Einstein's ..."

"Forget theories," Adam said. "Jack threw a car into a building by lifting his hand!"

"I agree with Sarah, let's wait for him to talk about it when he's ready."

"Let's get out of here first and sort everything else later," Frank said. "If Adam can stop long enough, I want everyone to know you did a good job back there."

"Everyone buckle up, the ride might be a little bumpy until we clear all the smoke and debris," Sarah said.

"So you're my son's college professor... and... you're a part–time pilot? How does that work?" Frank asked Sarah.

"It's a long story," Sarah said."

"Well, we've got a couple of hours to spare," Frank laughed. "I could use a long story, how about you?"

Sarah nodded. She answered questions for the first few minutes, mostly about her service in the military. As it turns out, they knew some of the same people. Frank seemed to know everybody, she thought to herself. He was amusing and extremely charming. Jack and his father were different. She could see how that might make communication challenging for them. But Sarah didn't mind telling Frank about her family and her life. He reminded her, in many ways, of her dad, the way he told jokes and his optimistic view on life. She enjoyed Frank's company. He was a good listener – he didn't judge, and he laughed with his eyes. He had a way of making you feel at ease, all the while, you're spilling embarrassing childhood moments ... teenage drama scenes ... and heart-breaking chapters in your life that you thought you'd never live through. They continued to talk endlessly, ignoring the other passengers.

"My father was military, so I was used to moving around," Sarah said. "That was our life, until he passed away. It shattered my world for a while...it took some time to find all the pieces. Military was my father's dream. After a while, I dreamed a new dream – I started teaching. I met Jack and here I am, following him around the world."

"He must have made quite an impression. Jack can be very eloquent and exciting when he makes an effort," Frank said, smiling.

"He is his father's son. I think you are both equally and masterfully charming."

"Thank you," he said, winking.

"See what I mean," Sarah laughed heartily. "The Prince men just can't help themselves. Women of the world, beware!"

Jack joined them in the pilot seats. He kneeled next to his dad and patted him on the back.

"Is everything all right in here," Jack asked. "You are having too much fun, I'm getting nervous. He's not showing you naked baby pictures of me, is he?"

"Your father has been on his very best behavior. He has only said kind things about you – nothing embarrassing ...yet," Sarah laughed.

"Things are fine son. I like her," Frank said, pointing at Sarah.

"Thanks dad, but I saw her first," Jack said, returning to his seat beside Adam.

"Are you going to talk about what happened or not?" Ivy tried to whisper. "Honestly, I don't see what the big deal is. Powers are cool, in my opinion. What's not to like?"

"I'm just trying to figure it out," he said.

"What do you have to figure out? This is a good thing, right Jack?" she said, forming the comment into a question.

"I'm not sure of anything. I don't have an answer for you right now. I don't know what I think about it," Jack said, quietly. "I just want to sit here and look out the window for a while."

"Sure," Ivy said. "I really just wanted to say that you're the same person, you know? Don't get all weird or anything. It's a cool thing. I just wanted you to know that."

"It happened so fast. I'll be fine," he reassured her. "I just want to process it more before I try to explain it to somebody else."

The new discovery had everyone buzzing with curiosity. There were whispers of the spectacular and frightening event. Everyone left Jack alone, but they talked nonstop about it in hushed tones.

"Where do we go from here?" Adam said. "What is as exciting as what just happened?"

"Wow," Ivy said. "Who knew that behind that technology hardware was a thrill seeker?"

"Is he going to be all right?" Finch asked, pointing at Jack.

"Yeah, he'll be fine," Adam said. "It's just that, he's a hard-nosed pragmatist. He's always thought that tragedy and ruin followed happy events – so he's waiting for the other shoe to drop. It is difficult for him to see this as something good happening in his life because he is already anticipating something bad following. Give him time … he'll snap out of it."

Jack ignored his friends' conversations. He heard them talking, but nothing seemed to make a difference, so he kept quiet. Instead, he pointed his hands toward a helmet in the corner and lifted the helmet in the air, moving it back and sent it spiraling into the chopper wall.

"Spectacular! I can actually hear the electrical residue," Finch said. "That was amazing. I'd love to document the research. Or are we still pretending not to talk about it."

"Is everyone alright?"

"Everyone's fine," Finch said. "Stop worrying."

"Can we talk about something else?" Jack said, quietly.

"Ok, what do think about the economic climate right now?" Ivy said sarcastically. "What do you mean, let's talk about something else? Really?"

"Well whatever it is, it sounds phenomenal, but if you don't want to talk about – we're fine with that," Finch said, looking in Ivy's direction.

"For now," she said under her breath, "I'll just listen to music and ignore Finch."

He smiled to himself, not bothering to respond.

"Jack, I don't think these guys are going to stop coming after you. If you and Frank decide that you need help or anything let me know. I'm here," Adam said. "But these guys were pretty serious; they spent a lot of time and effort over the years studying Frank's research – They took huge risks going after him. It's not likely that they will drop it just because of one bad day. I don't want to bring anyone down – I just want us to keep an eye out. This may not be over."

"I thought about that too," Jack said. "I'm not overlooking anything, but for now, we're safe. You guys should probably keep your distance for a couple of days while Frank and I figure out what's going on. The police will have questions for us about the mess we just left. I'd like to try to keep you guys out of it, if I can."

"What are you going to tell them about your powers or whatever that was?" Ivy asked, removing her headphones. "I tried not to listen, but I obviously failed."

"Nothing," Jack said. "At least I'm not telling them anything until I know more about it myself and I would appreciate if you guys didn't say anything about it either."

"I didn't see anything," Finch laughed. "Ivy, why don't you come over here and keep me company. I think I'd feel better if you sat next to me. I promise to be on my best behavior."

"Are you trying to change the subject," Ivy asked.

"Yes." Finch smiled. "I also invited you to join me."

Adam and Jack laughed at Ivy's discomfort over Finch's comments.

"I would be careful if I were you, Finch. Did you see the way she body slammed that one guard? He is going to need rehabilitative therapy, I bet," Adam joked. "And then, when she flipped that other guard and stomped him –she leapt onto that man's chest and flew into the air. She's dangerous."

"We get it, Adam. We were there, remember?" Ivy said.

"Wait. You guys don't understand," Finch said. "That's what I like about her. She's not a pushover. She's smart, attractive and adventuresome. It's a lethal combination – I love it."

"Okay, please, stop talking about me like I'm not here. No, thank you Finch, I'm fine sitting where I am."

"I'm blind. What are you afraid of?" he asked casually.

"You have a huge ego, do you know that?" Ivy said. "And don't try that innocent routine ... you see better than any one man should," she added.

"I'm going to take that as a compliment, coming from you," Finch said. "I just thought we had something going on – chemistry. I thought you might like to talk," he said.

"No. I would not like to talk about anything like that ...yet."

"Did I say something wrong," Finch asked.

Ivy didn't think Finch said anything wrong, but she was having a difficult time separating her excitement over rescuing Jack's dad, running out of burning buildings and the feelings that she and Finch had while they were fighting the guards in Texas. It was overwhelming and she didn't want to put her foot in her mouth and say something she might later regret. It was a lot to handle at one time.

"Don't take this personally," Ivy told Finch. "But I'm ignoring you for the rest of the flight. I just need to think about some things first, if you don't mind."

"Wow," Finch said. "Why would I take that personally?"

"You have misunderstood me," Ivy said.

"You could always explain," he said.

"I'm just not sure what to make of you yet. I can't tell when you're joking and when you're serious. I never know if you're humoring me or making fun of me. I like to observe people first."

Ivy waited for him to respond. When he didn't say anything, she kept talking.

"I'd like us to be friends. I just don't want to be one of those girls whose head is filled with flattery and compliments and regrets it later. This is an unusual situation we're in. There's enough fantastic drama in the air already without *this*."

"I understand," Finch said.

Ivy replaced her earphones and listened to music for the rest of flight.

"I don't understand her at all," Finch sighed.

"Why did you tell her you *did* understand?" Adam asked.

"That's what any good friend would have said."

Adam shrugged. He took his pillow and curled up near the window and tried to sleep.

"We're landing," Sarah yelled. "Stay seated until we've fully stopped."

As soon as the helicopter landed, everyone jumped out of their seats, hopping to the ground as the plane slowed to a crawl.

"It's just like being in class," Sarah told Frank. "Nobody listens to me."

"I spoke to Agent Powell and she is going to send a cleanup team to Texas. She wants to meet with me to get ahead of this before the press gets wind of it," Frank told the group. "Again, I just want to thank you all for what you did for Jack."

Sarah and Jack stood silent for a while looking awkwardly at each other.

Frank cleared his throat at the awkward silence. "I have a car waiting for me. I will see you at home, Jack."

"I'm sure I'll be seeing more of you," Frank told Sarah, giving her a hug. "I'm glad Jack has you for a friend."

"Thank you," she said. "It was the most fun I've had in a long time."

"Hey son thanks for coming after me," Frank whispered to Jack.

Frank nodded to them both, then turned and waved goodbye, as he walked to his car. Finch and Adam left with Ivy, leaving only Jack and Sarah.

"Um, I don't want to take advantage of the situation, but I sure am glad that you're safe ... and that you're here with me," Jack said.

"I'm a big girl" Sarah said, anticipating his next move. She leaned closer to him, until there was no space between them.

Jack took her hand and held it near his heart. With his other hand, he trailed down her shoulder to her elbow and leaned in even closer. Jack wasn't sure what Sarah's expectations were of him, but he wanted her to know that he hoped for something more. Neither of them spoke – they just stood holding each other, enjoying the feeling of victory.

In the distance, Jack could hear Frank's car driving off. He looked up as the black Aston Martin circled the black tarp and headed for the exit. Next, there was a loud explosion. The unimaginable, most unthinkable happened. Jack and Sarah took a staggering step toward the burning flames. Frank's car had blown up. As if in slow motion, the sound enveloped them…fumes and smoke covered the car.

"No," Jack whispered, falling to the ground. "No... no," he repeated.

This was too cruel a joke, Jack thought. "This isn't happening, he said. "It can't be – It can't be happening," Jack repeated over and over again.

Sarah stood there with him, horror-stricken and stunned. There were no words in existence to make this tolerable. He thought something bad would happen and it did. She wasn't sure what this would do to him … if anything would be right for him again. Her heart sank for him. She stayed there with him. He was inconsolable and momentarily lost. Sarah thought she heard a scream, she wasn't sure. Little could be heard above the explosive aftermath and Jack seemed unable to move. They had come so very far, to Hell and back to rescue his dad only to end up with this senseless act. Everything faded into nothingness. They sat there in the dark with no remembrance of the time.

CHAPTER 15

The memorial was small. It was a routine military service for someone of Frank's status. There were a lot of faces and speeches...all forgettable and unremarkable, Jack thought. Everyone was being overly polite and sympathetic, which did little to make sense of the loss. People hovered, nervously as if being alone was a bad thing all of a sudden.

"How are you Jack," Agent Powell asked. "I'm sorry for your loss."

"Thanks," he said.

"I'm just so truly sorry for you. If you find that you want to talk, don't hesitate to call me. Let me know if there is anything that I can do." She waited for a reply, and then searched for something appropriate to say.

"Let me assure you that we will continue with Frank's work. I can't pretend to know what you are going through but know that I am here. You can talk to me. Frank was a good agent. He has given us all hope."

"Thank you" Jack said, responding incoherently. He didn't even look at Agent Powell as he walked away mindlessly. Jack went through the motions, nodding his head and smiling. He did that a lot...smile – not really feeling anything.

Throughout the day, people, whose names he could no longer remember, paraded through the door, bringing food and offering words that did little, to fill the loss. Everything seemed a loss. The mourners in black ... *"the mourners in black, with their grief-filled snacks,"* he hummed. The phrase sounded like the words to a mindless song on the radio.

"Jack, are you all right?" Adam appeared. "Of course, you're not all right", he answered himself. "I just meant that you look tired, if I can say that."

"I'm fine," Jack said.

"Hi Jack," Finch and Ivy said together.

"Thanks guys for making the arrangements," Jack said. "It's like a revolving door in here. As soon as someone leaves, three more people arrive."

"Be nice. They're being respectful of Frank's memory," Ivy said, punching Finch lightly with her elbow. "We can hang around afterwards, too, if you need us. We can make sure the food gets to the kitchen and say the hellos and goodbyes."

"No, you guys can take off," Jack said.

"We're staying," Adam said. "Thanks for taking us up on our offer."

Jack sighed and walked away to Frank's study.

"We'll hang out and clean up," Ivy said. "Don't worry about a thing."

"Jack, are you sure you're all right?"

"I'm fine," he said, waving Adam away. His focus was on Haley.

"Fine, you can have your space today, Jack – but we are staying," Adam said, leaving him alone in the room.

"Haley, come here, girl." Jack opened the compartment on Haley's back. Inside was a sheet of paper. He didn't remember ever seeing the paper before. It contained the handwritten formula for the battery cell. It was his dad's handwriting, Jack noted. Jack ran his hand over the smooth paper. Just below the recipe for the formula was a personal note. It said, *"For safe keeping, love Frank."*

Jack stared at the letter for a while not knowing what to think. He glared at the glowing light inside Haley's battery compartment. "He made Haley's battery using his formula," Jack whispered. "It never needs charging."

Jack didn't notice that Agent Powell was quietly standing at the door. She backed away and quickly left without a word.

"Everyone is finally gone," Ivy said. "We're going to clean up and then we'll leave…unless you want company."

"Honestly, I want to be alone. Thank you. Tell the others I said thank you," Jack said. "I promise to call you if things get too weird."

The lifeless parade of people in black with that look on their faces that said, "you poor thing," was over. He relaxed his face and unglued the smile that had been stuck in place ever since the first mourner entered the room. It was over, he thought. The need to talk to people he didn't know and who didn't know him, was over. He no longer had to pretend. He liked the silence.

"It's just not fair," Jack thought. It made no sense that Frank should die over a battery. The more he thought about it the angrier he got. The angrier he got, the more set on revenge he became. He wanted someone to pay for this. Someone needed to pay for his father's death if it was the last thing he did, it would happen. He didn't care how long it took. It wasn't fair that he should keep losing people. His mother and now father were both sacrificed, for money and power.

Jack's rage grew and it filled him until it flowed outside of his body. He burned inside and his eyes flamed. He used his mind to lift the kitchen knives into the air and sent them flying at the wall. His aim was good and his strength was growing. The knives went through the wall into the next room, hitting the dart board. The release felt good. Jack decided to start exercising his energies on getting stronger. He felt a battle coming his way and he wanted to be ready.

CHAPTER 16

It was sunrise. Sarah found herself jogging farther than her usual four miles. She was listening to music on her ear phones, losing herself in thought about Jack. As she continued to run and listen to the music, the images of Jack grew stronger. She was barely conscious of passing all of her usual stops – and was now going outside her neighborhood. Sarah ran faster. Her excitement grew and the images of Jack become even stronger. The air held an electric charge as she pushed herself to go farther and farther and then, she was suddenly aware that she was on the street where Jack lived. She had been running to Jack. The thought made her giddy and a new energy surged through her body as she ran.

It was early morning. The neighborhood was still asleep; there was no movement at all on the streets.

The corner stores were not open yet. It was still quiet. The weather was warm already and the air salty. There was little breeze that pushed Sarah forward, giving her courage. From down the street, a dark-colored van, inconspicuously parked, was monitoring Jack's house. The mysterious man inside the van made a call.

"He's still at home. No, he rarely leaves," the man said ducking down. He watched Sarah jogging and paused. "Yes I understand, completely," he said. "I am only supposed to watch and not to approach him. See what he does and follow him. I've got it."

"I still think I should try to get in and plant listening devices," he said to himself."

When the man saw Sarah at Jack's door, he ducked down even farther. The man had seen Finch, and Adam visit on occasion, but no one else. He noticed Sarah London at the door. He made notes about her in his book, so that he could report back to the office. The man inside the van reached down and grabbed his camera. He began taking random photos of Sarah as he watched the encounter.

"Who are you?" he asked himself, taking bites of his sandwich, in between leering. "I wonder what you will be talking about?" He kept taking pictures of Sarah until she entered the house. "One thing I can say is that the man has taste, that's for sure." He looked at his watch and took a few more notes and then reclined back in his seat. He continued to eat his sandwich and waited for Sarah to come out.

Sarah jumped a little when Jack opened the door.

"Hi Sarah, it's good to see you," he said. "Come in."

"Hi, is it all right that I'm here?" she asked.

"You're welcome anytime," he said, standing to the side, allowing her to enter.

Sarah stood hesitantly outside the door before entering. She didn't know what to say and wondered what excuse she had for coming by unannounced. She was, after all, technically his college professor and things were already complicated enough. But, he had not been attending class, so that would be a legitimate reason to stop by...a professional reason to stop by. Although, in her heart, she knew the truth, which was that she just wanted to see Jack and to be near him and she wanted to know that he was okay.

She knew it would be inappropriate to tell him these things, but inside she missed seeing him. It would probably go to his head anyway, she told herself. Any indication of desperation on her part would likely fill his head bigger, if that was even possible. Sarah was sure that Jack had never experienced rejection from a girl. He surely had no problem meeting women – they probably threw themselves at him all the time and why not? Jack was handsome, she thought. He was rich, too and that never hurt. Jack was extremely smart and he had that whole superhuman superman power thing going on, which was pretty freaking awesome if she had to say so, herself.

"Sarah, come in, please," Jack pressed. "Did you run all the way here, just to stand on my porch?"

"Thank you. I was running in the neighborhood," Sarah said.

"Lucky me," Jack said. "You are always welcome. I mean that, sincerely." He reached out and took hold of her hand and pulled her gently inside.

"Well, you haven't been to class, and I was wondering if you were all right," Sarah said, which was every bit the truth. She looked around the house. It was overflowing with papers surrounding his dad's work and replete with information on Sector Twelve. She could see that Jack appeared to be overly preoccupied, consumed even, with avenging his dad's murder instead of moving forward. She was more worried than before. Was he eating? She could tell that he wasn't sleeping. He looked tired.

"Jack what are you doing? Sarah asked, hurriedly. "You don't look like you're sleeping. You're probably not eating enough. What are you doing with all this?" She picked up the papers overflowing the table. "Why not let the FBI or CIA or whoever take care of this? It will consume you until there's nothing left. That can't be what your father would have wanted for you."

Jack looked at Sarah in her running outfit and took her hand. He acted as if she hadn't said anything. He pulled her close to him and held her, gazing into her eyes.

"Be serious, Jack," she smiled, completely melting away any frustration.

"I'm very serious," he said, never moving his eyes away from hers. "I think you're seriously cute. Have you come to distract me?"

"No, but… is it working? Am I distracting?" Sarah joked with Jack. She liked it when he was playful.

"I can't remember anything but you. When you're near me – nothing else exists; there is only you. You fill my thoughts completely and there isn't space for anything except you. I could live forever in this one moment with you." Jack searched Sarah's eyes and wondered what she was thinking. He held her as he spoke and was glad that she didn't pull away. She was beginning to allow herself to trust him. The thought pleased Jack.

Jack decided that he didn't want to worry Sarah. He would not discuss going after his father's killers while they were together, but there was no way that he was going to stop trying to find out more about who killed his dad.

"So, why haven't you been to class, Jack?" You're not even keeping in touch with your friends – I know, Jack. I see Ivy and Adam at school and they're concerned as well."

Sarah didn't mean to sound preachy and she didn't want Jack upset but she didn't want him to sit in the house all day devising a strategy that could get him killed. Sarah wanted to tell Jack that she was worried about him, but the words wouldn't come.

"I'd rather we went back to talking about how very attractive you look and that I'm glad you stopped by – you're a very good distraction," Jack said. He squinted his eyes and used his mind to pull Sarah closer to him and he put his arm around her back.

"Well, I see you've been practicing. Your powers seem stronger," she smiled, trying to concentrate on something other than his hand curved around her back. "I understand that you've been having a difficult time and I thought you might need to talk to someone about what's going on."

"I'm fine," Jack said. "Stop worrying." He leaned forward and kissed her forehead lightly – continuing further to kiss the base of her throat. And then, he paused, allowing his lips to travel slowly, skimming her throat and just holding her.

Sarah was uncharacteristically quiet. Jack leaned back to look in her eyes when she didn't respond. She stared back at him.

"Why did you say you stopped by?" he asked, holding her softly.

Jack smiled, and continued to stare at Sarah until she finally spoke.

"I just want to know that you're doing well," Sarah said, looking up into Jack's piercing eyes.

"I told you, I'm fine."

"I heard you the first time, Jack," she said, trying to put some distance between them but Jack held on tighter.

"Well, I am fine and I feel even better now having you here." Jack focused and used his power to propel her forward again so that she was pressed against him.

"No fair," Sarah said, but she didn't try to move away. If she were truthful with herself, she would admit that she didn't mind Jack's games. She was all too willing to play along, *for a while.*

Sarah stared at Jack, wanting to empty her heart to him but knowing this was not the right time. He was too preoccupied with the way he was holding her to process anything. But she took advantage of the moment to enjoy the nearness of him and how good he felt. She was breathing stronger now and she wondered if Jack could tell.

"What are we doing Jack?" she asked, breathlessly.

"You're distracting me, remember?" Jack said as he leaned closer to kiss Sarah's neck.

Sarah leaned her head back to allow Jack to kiss her and she inhaled sharply. She closed her eyes as he held her. Sarah wanted to remain detached and focused but it was hard to do when she was standing so close to him.

"Jack, I should be going, now. I just wanted to stop by to make sure things were okay, since you're still not coming to school."

"You can't go yet," Jack said as he lifted Sarah's hand and kissed the inside of her palm. "We're not through with my tutoring session. He continued kissing Sarah's arm and then the inside of her elbow and the top of her shoulder and then her chin.

"I admit that I'm having fun with you, but there can't be anything real between us while you're battling whatever this is," she said pointing to the papers. "You have too many pots in the fire. You have too much unfinished business. I can't tell that you're certain of anything, except that fact that you want revenge. But, there are other things in life, Jack. If you quit so easily ... well, I can't see that as a positive thing."

"I see. You think I'm neglecting responsibility, is that it? You sound a little like my father," he admitted.

"I'm simply asking, *what are you doing*? You could give me a simple answer."

"I don't know," Jack said.

"Clearly, you're gifted, but that seems to have no effect on you. You're alarmingly attractive – you're funny – but you're a horrible communicator and you're willing to hide away here in your castle. What you are doing doesn't make sense to me. I like my life to make sense. I like order and structure. I like playing by the rules."

"Before I met you, my life fit very neatly in a pristine, identifiable box," she said, choosing her words carefully. "I guess I'm not very good with spontaneous, knock your socks off, surprises, that's all. This is all much more complicated than I thought." Sarah stood straighter and lifted her head. "So, you will you forgive me, please, when I say that I don't think you are prioritizing things well. I just wanted to pass that along."

"I see." Jack listened, watching her intently as she spoke.

"You're not by yourself – you have friends," she said in a more softened tone. "Why don't you let them help? It's not a weakness to ask for help, Jack. There's room for more than one star."

"This is not about being the star – this is about trying to keep the people that I care about safe. This is my life, the good, the bad and the totally insane – all of it. It's too much to expect anyone else to take this kind of chaos on – plus, I know what I'm doing – I can handle things."

"Well, you're neglecting your classes, your friends, your father's company…

"I kind of have other things on my mind right now, Sarah," Jack said annoyed.

"Really, Jack," Sarah replied. "What was your excuse before?" You cannot let life sidetrack you."

She drew her fist into a tight ball. "Be mad, yell, hit the wall, but keep going!"

"You can't understand," he said, turning away from her.

"What? You don't think that I can understand that life stinks sometimes?" Sarah asked. "Just when you think you're moving forward, you get the rug pulled out from under you! I can understand getting kicked in the gut by forces you can't control. I get it."

Jack stood silently still. He wouldn't look at Sarah.

You're still doing it, you know… shutting yourself off. That's what you do – you've gotten pretty good at it. We choose our paths, Jack. I understand better than you think; only I'm not a quitter." Sarah turned and walked out.

Just outside the door, she paused. She started to turn around and go back in and apologize to Jack, but decided that she was right. If they had any chance of anything in the future, she had to be honest with him, even if it made him angry.

"Breathe, she said to herself. "Stay in control and be firm" she repeated as she put her earphones back on and continued her run. She was happy to put as much distance as possible between them. The brisk air would do wonders to clear her head. So, she ran, giving herself over to the run and the sounds of Justin Timberlake playing on her iPod.

Part of her regretted the words she said to Jack – her other half knew that it was exactly what he needed to hear. She knew exactly what he was going through and the difficult time he was having. It was the same as her experience when her father died, but she did not want him to get lost in his grief. She was not an insensitive person. She knew first-hand that grief was a magnet of emotions pulling you in every direction. She remembered the days after her father's death – how completely lost and out of control she felt until she allowed her friends to pull her back from the edge. So she knew that too much solitude wasn't good for Jack. She decided that she would find a way to help him, whether he wanted it or not – she would force it on him and enlist his friends. It would be a challenge, she thought because she had made up her mind that Jack was just as stubborn as she was. "But, I'm up for the challenge," she said to herself.

Back inside the house, Jack exploded — or rather the kitchen appliances exploded. Jack did not want to admit that maybe Sarah was right and that he was letting his emotions get to him...being ruled by them. The noise from the explosion made Haley run and crouch behind his leg.

"Sorry, girl," Jack exhaled.

He took a few deep breaths and bent down to pet Haley.

"Some guard dog you turned out to be," Jack said smiling.

He picked up the remote control and clicked in Haley's direction, changing her image into a poodle, then a Doberman, a bloodhound and finally back into a golden, chestnut colored, Finnish Spitz.

"I guess you're perfect just the way you are," he said, petting Haley.

Sarah entered her house after finishing her run. She was preoccupied, still very frustrated after her conversation with Jack that she didn't notice the dark van sitting outside her driveway. Sarah entered the front door, and flipped on the lights. She went to the kitchen and sat at the counter to think. The doorbell rang and she got up and started walking toward the door. She heard a noise behind her and turned around. She didn't recognize the man standing in her room – she opened her mouth to scream but was hit in the back of the head. She fell forward and hit the floor. The men stood over her for a few seconds –staring at her unconscious body. One of the men gathered rope and began tying her hands and feet. The other man surveyed the room, trying to make sure nothing was out of place.

"Don't hurt her," the man said. "We were paid to retrieve the girl only. Half the money for the pickup and the other half for delivery; those are the terms. She does not get hurt....at least not yet," he said.

The other man peeped through the curtains and said, "Come on. We're wasting time. Let's go before someone sees us."

They picked Sarah up and waited for the driver to back the van closer to the door. They couldn't take a chance on someone seeing them and involving the police.

The van from the street backed into the driveway. The man carried Sarah over his shoulder and dumped her in the back of the van. She was completely unconscious as they drove away. The driver handed a phone to the man sitting in the passenger seat, "Inform the boss that we have the girl and we're on our way in."

CHAPTER 17

Adam and Finch arrived at the university concert hall. They pushed through the crowd, weaving in and out of friends and family trying to find seats for the concert. Adam found two available seats just as the orchestra began to play. Adam and Finch looked around on stage at the orchestra and then down at the program.

"Ivy has a solo up next," Adam said.

"Did you tell her we were coming?" Finch asked softly, trying not to disturb the people sitting next to them.

"Well...she's been so busy getting ready for this concert that I didn't have time. What was I going to do, call her and say Finch and I think we know who killed Frank but we're not sure if we should tell Jack because he's already half-crazy that we think it will send him over the edge?"

"So, she doesn't know we're here?" Finch asked, half laughing, while tossing jelly beans into his mouth.

"No."

"How long is this going to take? Are you planning on sitting through the entire concert?"

"Shh," the man behind them hissed.

Adam ignored Finch and continued to listen to the song. Every now and then, Adam would try to hush Finch. People were beginning to stare because he was talking a lot during the music. Adam didn't like classical music and the symphony seemed an otherwise boring way to spend an afternoon, but he did, however, look forward to seeing Ivy and of course, he knew that Finch would jump at any occasion to see her, too, although he would not admit it.

The music swelled loudly and Adam's focus went to the stage. Everyone was dressed in black tie for the occasion. The men wore tuxedos and the girls had on fancy black dresses and high heels. It was a nice change from the jeans and flip flops that the girls wore every day. He had never seen Ivy play on stage before and he had also never seen her in a dress, so this was exciting, despite his dislike for the symphony.

"What are they playing? What is this music, anyway?" Adam asked as he opened the program.

"Johann Bach's Chaconne," Finch said, smirking.

"How do you know that?" Adam said, giving him a sharp elbow to his side.

"Dude, I have a very sophisticated ear," he answered mockingly.

"Since when?" Adam asked, with a hint of disbelief.

"Since I found out that Ivy was into classical music – that's since when. I do my homework. Take notes." Finch laughed too loudly and the audience members hushed them again.

From back stage, Ivy paced nervously. She was always nervous before a performance, so this was nothing new. She had techniques that she used to slow down her breathing and calm herself – so she wouldn't panic and do something embarrassing, like faint or throw up or something equally lame. She did some breathing exercises to slow her heartbeat.

"You will be great. You will remember every note and be fantastic. They're going to love you." She repeated the words again, telling herself over and over until her confidence grew.

Ivy walked closer to the stage so she could take a peek at the audience. She was a little disappointed that her parents couldn't attend, but it was a long, expensive flight and she understood. They had heard her many times, but somehow it wasn't quite the same without her family in the audience. They promised to fly into the country for her next performance. As Ivy surveyed the audience, she saw Adam and Finch.

"What are *they* doing here?" Ivy asked herself in barely a whisper.

Ivy put her violin down on the table and picked up a straw and napkin. She tore little pieces of the napkin and inserted it into the straw. She laughed at the absurdity of her act, but decided to do it anyway. She took a deep breath and began sending napkin spit balls hurling into the audience, targeting Adam and Finch. She giggled and then paused as the first couple of balls hit the couple in front of Adam. Ivy dodged behind the curtain and started again. This time, she corrected her aim and took another breath and aimed at Finch.

"Bingo," she said and smiled when Adam looked her way.

A spitball spiraled toward Finch and without a word, he lifted his hand and grabbed the spit ball and smiled.

"I think Ivy has spotted us," Adam said laughing.

The orchestra played softly and Ivy walked on stage for her solo. The audience applauded as she took her place center stage. There was a long pause and then Ivy lifted her violin and began to play. Her arm moved back and forth quickly as the notes became second nature. She anticipated and played each note with ease and confidence.

"What is she wearing?" Finch asked.

"A black dress," Adam said.

"Is it tight?" Finch asked.

"You're sick dude. She is wearing a dress – she looks nice."

He thought she looked more than nice and should wear more dresses but he would never dare tell her that unless he wanted to get thrown into a wall or tackled.

Ivy continued to play, slowing and then changing tempo. Adam was impressed. It was not his kind of music but he did appreciate the complexity involved and thought she was amazing. When Ivy finished, the audience gave her a standing ovation, including Finch. As she walked off stage, the orchestra continued playing more songs. Adam and Finch got up and headed back stage to see her.

Adam led Finch, weaving in and out of stage handlers, directors and crewmen until he found Ivy. She almost jumped into Adam's arms.

"So, how was I? Spectacular right! Go ahead, you can tell me!" Ivy said with great excitement.

"You were amazing," Adam said truthfully. "You made me love the symphony and that is a miracle. You look pretty amazing, too," Adam said.

"Let *me* get some compliments in," Finch said. "I thoroughly enjoyed your solo. It was brilliant. I imagined all kinds of delicious and wicked things as you played. It was perfect, and I should know. I have highly-sensitive ears."

He had been to the symphony a couple of times before and always by force because a girl he was dating would drag him with her. But this was different. Number one, he was actually very interested in Ivy and number two, he was interested in whatever interested Ivy.

"Nice catch, by the way," she said, trying not to laugh.

"I'm a willing target anytime, however, I think you freaked out that poor couple in front of us," Finch said.

"Well, thank you both for coming to my performance, but I can't help thinking that your attendance is not due to your love for the arts. So, what chaos has been unleashed that would drag the two of you hard rockers to a symphony?"

Adam and Finch looked at each other before speaking.

"Guys, I'm getting older by the minute. Spill it."

Adam said, "Fine. Take a look at this."

He showed her the document with the names of the leaders of Sector Twelve.

"We never completed looking at all the names once we located the spot where Frank was being held, but see, here."

Ivy looked at the document and paused. The symphonic band was still playing in the background. She took a few steps away from the sound to concentrate on the document. Her eyes focused as she put together the dots. She slowly began to catch up.

"Agent Powell is one of the Twelve! We have to tell Jack," she said.

"Whoa," Adam said. "Slow down."

"What do you mean whoa?" Ivy asked.

"Well, Jack is a little crazy right now, so...," Adam trailed off.

"What do you mean?" She was looking at them as if they just said something like the world was flat. She said the next words very slowly as if talking to a two year old, "We – Have – To – Tell – Jack," she sighed. "What is it with guys and communication?"

"Wait here while I get changed and we'll tell him together." Ivy turned and quickly slapped Finch on the bottom

"Don't worry baby, I'll protect you," she said, laughing.

"I'm in" Finch said.

They waited out front, leaving the melody of the symphonic band behind.

"She likes me, right?" Finch asked.

"I don't know," Adam said. "Leave me out of it."

They all descended on Jack's doorstep. Ivy was in front and the boys were hanging behind to feel out his mood. They felt that he would relate better to Ivy – less likely to send a girl flying through the door in anger. They could hear Haley barking through the other side of the door. She rang the doorbell again.

Jack opened the door and looked at the group. He shook his head, smiling.

"Come in. Don't tell me. You were all just in the neighborhood."

"Not exactly," Ivy said. "We found out that Agent Powell is one of the leaders in Sector Twelve and we all think she is behind Frank's accident."

"Just blurt it out then," Finch said.

Adam took out the paper and showed it to Jack.

"I found out that she is no longer active in the agency. She was suspended because they suspected her of trading weapons for US secrets," Finch said.

Haley went underneath the table and put her head down as the foundation began to shake. Everyone braced themselves for the eruption, but very soon, the shaking stopped and Jack relaxed.

"I'm fine guys. I'll take it from here," he said.

"No, you won't. You can't do this by yourself and that little demonstration proves my point," Adam said, grabbing him by the shoulder.

"What's your point?" Jack wanted to know.

"You're not in the best frame of mind. We're worried that you are letting your emotions cloud your judgment and your powers...are not the most stable. Jack, this is still very new. You're not one of your father's designs that you toss to the side because it 'hasn't been tested,'" Adam scoffed.

"I'm not asking for anyone's permission on this," he said, looking at his friends. "I get that you're all concerned and I am glad that you are, but this is something that *I* have to do. I'm moving forward on this. It's not about revenge – it's about justice."

"I'll order the pizza, it's going to be a long night," Finch said, walking past them to the sofa.

Jack looked at the three people with him. He was actually glad they came to visit and glad they offered support that he never would have asked for and not likely would have taken a few days ago. But, for what it was worth, he would allow them in to bring some civility and humanity back from the insanity that he was going through.

They moved and rearranged furniture from the center of the floor. Adam took out his computer, then put electrodes on Jack and let him run on the treadmill as he took notes. He leaned over to try to look at Adam's notes and he pressed the clipboard to his chest, "Eyes on the road," as he moved away back towards his computer.

"You're fast," Adam said. "You're not faster than a speeding bullet or anything like that – it's more strength. Why didn't I think of that before — it's Newton's Second Law of Motion. Force equals mass times acceleration. So, try it – the same way you maneuver energy, should push you faster."

Jack ran faster and faster until smoke started coming from the machine, causing electrical sparks – which sent Haley running from the room. Adam began drawing a series of formulas on a projector and explaining the equations as Jack ran on the treadmill. The first set of formulas dealt with speed and Adam rambled on and on regarding kinetic energy, motion, and velocity.

"There is a direct relationship between matter and energy, which we learned from Einstein Theory of Relativity formula," Adam said. He took a bucket of golf balls and placed them center room. He looked at his friend and laughed.

"Are you ready?" Adam raised an eyebrow and slowly picked up the golf balls.

"What are you doing?" Jack asked.

He didn't respond, but extended his arm backward and began to throw the ball directly at the treadmill.

Jack watched as the balls release from Adam's hand. The ball accelerated and he raised his hand until the ball slowed and finally stopped a few inches away from his face and dropped to the floor.

"Are you trying to kill me?" Jack asked.

"Every action has an equal and opposite reaction – it's Newton's Third Law. Try again," Adam commanded Jack. This time, he tossed all three of the balls at Jack.

"On the count of three, guys – one – two – three," Adam instructed.

They all threw balls toward Jack, as instructed. It only took a second to focus and slow the acceleration of the balls and then redirect them. The balls started to spin in a circle, spiraling uniformly until they flew through the window, shattering glass and car windows.

"I think that went well. That's enough for the day," Jack said.

While Adam talked about theories, Ivy and Finch played around on the other side of the room. Ivy practiced her karate moves on Finch. He dodged and ducked on cue to avoid being completely massacred by her strength.

"Time out," Finch breathed. "We have to find you a more suitable sparring partner."

He moved out of the way just as Ivy's foot crushed through the table.

"Now it's my turn," she told Jack, breathing heavily and taking a firm defensive stance.

"This is called the Indian Death Lock. You can use it against frontal attacks.

I'm going to need a volunteer – so come here, Adam," she said.

"Why is it always me? I have one request – please stay away from any vital organs that I may need in the future. This is only a simulation, right?" he said, grimacing.

"Follow closely," she said, ignoring Finch's comments. "As your attacker strikes, step forward and to the left slightly with your left foot and use a left-handed head block. Strike your attacker's right hip with your left hand and cup round the back of their right ankle with your right hand. Keeping your attackers right leg pinned, grab the left ankle with your right hand and strike the back of the knee with your left hand. Use your right hand to bring your attackers right ankle to your left hand. Now, this is the really cool part: place the edge of your left foot under your attackers chin and push away with your foot. Yeah, if they recover, facial reconstructive surgery is a must!"

"You are so deadly. I like it," Finch blurted with no feigned pretense. "You're the perfect combination of beauty and strength. I don't know whether to bow at your feet or run for my life."

Adam and Jack exchanged looks and fist pumped at Finch's moves. He definitely had 'a way' or 'skill' that neither of them possessed – maybe he practiced more, but whatever it was, he made it look easy. He had style. He had not let the fact that he was blind overshadow his other strengths. He was confident, maybe overly so – but it worked for him.

When Finch and Ivy decided to tour the house, Adam asked Jack about Professor London.

"So how are you and the teacher doing?" Adam asked, curiously.

It was a little awkward the whole teacher hanging out with the students thing but he was happy because it seemed that Jack really cared for her.

"Does she ask about me?" Jack questioned.

"No, actually, she has been absent for a few days. You should call her? Adam insisted.

Jack thought about it. He actually wanted to talk to Sarah but he didn't know what to say and he really wanted to let this craziness pass before saying anything. The truth is that he was scared. Jack was scared of what Sarah was beginning to mean to him. Jack was scared of losing someone else.

"No," Jack told Adam. "Maybe I will call her after we do this. I don't want her involved. Things didn't exactly work out last time."

"Jack, your father's death was not your fault. Frank was an FBI agent – he woke up and slept in the presence of danger all the time. He had enemies, some more dangerous than others – but that's why he was so opposed to letting his designs get into the wrong hands. He didn't want the good work that he did to be controlled by evil people. He wanted to make the world safer – he wanted to use the battery to fuel hospitals in third-world countries and to help fuel cars to decrease pollution. He fought for it…for you, for your mom – for all of us. That's who he was. He made choices, but I don't think he would have changed one thing," Adam said.

"I know," Jack said. "It doesn't make any of this feel any better…it makes the whole thing seem that much more tragic."

"I think you could have seen that part of Frank, if you weren't so busy trying to blame someone, you know?" Adam said. "You have to let some of the unanswered questions go, so that you can move on."

"Can we talk about something else, now?" Jack sighed.

"I could give you some tips, you know. I could share my know–how about the ladies," he said, trying to lighten the mood. "Really…I could help you with the professor."

"Oh, by all means, share the '*know–how*,'" Jack said laughing. Adam could always be trusted to cheer him up. Adam, the bookworm could rarely be found outside the library or away from his chess game. But, girls liked the sweet, nerdy boy image. Adam was naturally fit, but no one would ever call him buff. He did, however make prep boy fashion seem chic. From what he had seen, Adam had no problem attracting girls, but they usually took a back seat to his academics, which Jack admired, but often told Adam he was crazy.

"Girls like funny," Adam said. "You should keep her laughing. Girls are always laughing at me."

"I can believe that," Jack said.

"Then, between laughs, I slip in and make my move. Works every time," Adam said. "Okay, so I know I'm not *that* funny, but that's what gets them. They feel sorry for me and think I'm cute when I'm trying to be funny. You should try it."

"Thanks for the advice. What do you suppose Ivy and Finch are up to?" Jack wanted to change the subject. Looking toward the other room, he raised an eyebrow. They shared a veiled look…"getting his butt kicked."

From the other side of the house, Ivy found a room that was adjacent to an outdoor garden deck – it was in the middle of two outside fountains next to an oversized pool with a waterfall. She had never seen anything so uniquely placed. It was almost sacred. She opened the double doors.   There was an oversized, well-placed garden to the right near an enclosed sauna room. She would have called it Eden – it looked like paradise. It was the most beautiful space she had seen, she thought to herself – it was perfect. Ivy and Finch walked around the room until he grabbed her hand.

"Wait a minute," Finch said. He took his hands and put them on either side of her face.

"What are you doing?" she asked.

"Confirming my suspicion," he said, smiling and caressing Ivy's face.

"Suspicion...," she breathed.

"That you're beautiful," Finch said, roughly.

Ivy dropped her hands down to her sides as he traced the outlines of her face. He gently moved his hands over her eyes, slowly letting his hand rest on her cheek, then, using his thumbs to trace the shape of her lips and he paused for what seemed like a lifetime.

"Finch," Ivy started to say something light to break the intensity, but he interrupted her.

"Shh," he said, as he continued his discovery. Her lips parted under his touch and he leaned closer, letting his senses lead him. Finch could not see Ivy, but he knew she was, "beautiful," he said out loud. One of his hands rested on her throat and he leaned closer until he was inches from her face.

Suddenly, Ivy stiffened. She was startled by a loud, very intrusive noise. Realization set in that they were not alone. The guys grinned and elbowed each other and grinned widely.

"What happened to you two?" they asked, shoving each other and trying to hold back the laughter that was building.

"I think I just lost a bet, "Adam said. "I'm ready to leave when you two are. Unlike some of you, I have an early class and I still have to study."

Finch and Ivy smiled at each other for a moment – but neither of them was in a hurry to move. They ignored Adam and Jack, finally, slowly releasing their gaze. They followed them, reluctantly out of the room.

"Paradise," Ivy whispered to herself. As she passed by Adam, she punched him in the arm.

"No jokes! Nothing happened," she said.

"That was definitely something," Finch said. "Actually, it was indescribable, wonder, and amazingly fantastic and unlike anything he had ever experienced and never wanted to forget.

Adam drove Ivy and Finch home. As they pulled up to Ivy's parking lot, Finch got out and walked around to open the car door for her. He walked her to the apartment door.

"I could come up with you, if you'd like," he said.

"Maybe another time," Ivy sighed. "Let's not read too much into this, okay. I don't want things to be weird."

Finch was unexpected – but way too confident. She liked confidence, but Finch had a way of making her feel like she was standing in front of him in her underwear – and he was blind. It was the craziest thing – but he made her feel like he could see the parts of herself that she kept hidden from the world.

"We passed weird two hours ago," Finch said. "Well, at the risk of making things weird ...," Finch leaned forward and kissed Ivy lightly on the lips. "I want to know everything about you, Ivy Cannon. My heart knows you already. The sound of our hearts together is music. Weird can be good."

"I don't know what to say to that," she said. "You always say the most breathtakingly stunning thing to make me forget what I was going to say."

"Thank you, I think," he said.

"Good night Finch."

"Goodnight," Finch said as he walked away.

"Okay, did she look at me as if she liked me?" he asked, closing the car door.

"I don't know," Adam said. "I told you to leave me out of this."

"But how was that? It felt good, could you tell?"

"Yeah, she was totally drooling. You are the man," Adam said, shaking his head.

"You're laughing at me, aren't you?" Finch asked.

"Yeah, I am laughing at you. You are completely going against the man code with all this sensitivity talk," Adam said. "Relax. You and Jack both are losing your minds over these girls. It's fine, but no more talk about feelings."

That was the end of the conversation. They drove down the street with music blaring until they arrived at Finch's house.

Finch got out of the car with a slight wave backward. He approached his garage and slowed as he reached the door. Something was off, he thought. Someone was here, waiting for him. A man jumped out of nowhere and swung, trying to punch Finch in the face. He ducked; kicking the man in what he hoped was his throat. Two men grabbed him from behind, but Finch was able to pick up a crowbar and used it to hit one man in the side and twisted around to leave the other man's shoulder twisted and mangled. Finch's elbow came down hard on the man's shoulder. He had an advantage over his attackers. He knew where everything was. He picked up and threw a wrench at the man in front of him, which broke his nose. He heard the bone crack and he felt some degree of satisfaction.

"Never sneak up on a blind guy!" Finch shouted at the men as they ran away. He soon realized that the men left because of a car coming down the street.

Finch stepped on something with his foot and reached over to pick up the cell phone that had been dropped on the floor by one of the men.

Back at Ivy's apartment, she smiled as she thought about Finch and everything that happened that day. She entered her apartment and turned on the lights. She removed her jacket and headed toward the bedroom when two men grabbed her. She broke one of their arms, then jumped feet first; crouching on the other's back, knocking him into a table. Suddenly, a cloth was over her face as she struggled to avoid breathing the chemical that was slowly taking over her senses. She stomped on the man's foot that was holding her but it was not enough to free herself. The room started spinning as she slumped over and was carried away.

"We've got the girl. Pick up the guy," the man in black said as he looked around the room. The three men left Ivy's apartment and put her into a van and drove away.

CHAPTER 18

The men drove until they arrived at the waterfront docks, then they put Ivy in a cart and wheeled her onto a boat. She was still unconscious as they sped farther away from the shore. The wind was strong against the speed boat and they kept checking to make sure that she was still asleep. They used binoculars to eye their target, which was a big, oversized yacht just ahead of them.

The men waved toward the yacht as they approached. They tied Ivy's hands and feet and prepared to pick her up and transport her to the yacht. When the boat was adjacent to the yacht, they carried her to the deck and then downstairs to one of the rooms. Two guards with guns stood at the door.

"We brought a guest," the man said, carrying Ivy. The two guards stepped aside.

"Let me out!" Sarah yelled from inside the room. "What do you want," she demanded. "Somebody tell me what's going on!"

The men dumped Ivy on the sofa inside the room with Sarah.

"Oh no! What did you do to her?" Sarah asked as the men left, completely ignoring her. "Ivy, wake up!"

Her hands were tied behind her back. Sarah scooted next to Ivy and nudged her until she regained consciousness. Ivy started to move and Sarah suddenly felt better.

"Ivy, are you all right?" Sarah asked as she saw that Ivy was beginning to focus on the room. Her eyes were no longer Drifting. "You're going to be okay," Sarah whispered.

"Professor?" Ivy whispered. "Where are we?"

She could feel that she was in restraints. Her memory was slowly coming back. A vision of the past few hours flashed in her mind. She had entered her apartment and was attacked and then she was floating. They had put some sort of chemical over her face and that was the last thing she remembered.

"I think it's fine that you call me Sarah outside of the classroom," she laughed at Ivy's discomfort. They had been through enough to be on a first-name basis.

"It's still a little weird. I'll get used to it, I suppose" Ivy said. It looks like we're going to be here for a while anyway. How long have we been here?" she asked.

"You just arrived. I've been here for a couple of days, Sarah told her. "Are you all right? Are you hurt?"

"No, I'm fine," Ivy said. "What do they want?"

"I don't know and they aren't talking. We are on a yacht in the middle of the ocean and now you know what I know," Sarah said. "I don't suppose you have a cell phone on you, by any chance?"

"No, we're out of luck, there," Ivy said. "Is there something that we can use to get out of these ropes?" The room was a boring beige color and devoid of character. There was very little furniture except for an oversized chair that Sarah was sitting in and two cots in the corner. This was not one of the guest quarters. They were locked in a storage room or maybe a servant's quarters.

"Wow, I've just been sitting here for three days and I haven't thought about trying to get free," Sarah said sarcastically.

Smiling, Ivy said, "The teacher's got a bit of an attitude! I didn't mean it like that; I just don't want to stick around for whatever these guys have in mind. You will excuse me if I'm thinking about kicking some butt and making a run for it."

"Have you looked out the portal?" Sarah asked. "We are on a boat in the middle of the ocean. Where are you going to run?"

Ivy didn't have a lot of patience and she really didn't like the idea of being held captive. She couldn't even understand how she let this happen in the first place – she was usually so much more aware and these guys didn't seem overly smart. Maybe she didn't have Sarah's sophistication, but as far as she was concerned, this really wasn't the time for passive aggression. "Have you looked around, Sarah? We are in serious trouble here. I'm thinking anyplace is better than this right now. I get that you're a 'wait around for your Prince to show kind of a girl,' but I am a 'take no prisoner, hit'em high and kick 'em low kind of a girl.'" Ivy started kicking her feet against the wall repeatedly. One of the guards unlocked the door and entered the room and Ivy charged him, even though her hands and feet were bound. She swung her arms like she was at batting practice and hit the man across the chest and flipped, kicking him in the most delicate of places. Three other men entered, guns cocked and jumped her from behind. One hit Ivy with the back of the gun and she fell on her back, looking face up at Sarah.

The corners of Sarah's mouth turned up…, "hmm, I think you said hit them high and kick them low – how's that working out for you?"

Knowing that she wasn't seriously hurt, made it easier for Sarah to laugh at the sight of her sprawled on her back with a look of embarrassment. Ivy did look pretty silly with her mouth gaped open from the shock. When all of this trouble was behind them, she could see her and Ivy becoming very good friends – that is, if she could get past the whole hanging out with a teacher thing.

The man said, "Now, sit down and shut up." He told the other men, who were standing behind him, to tie Ivy up – and, "real good this time." They tied her more securely and roped her feet at the ankles to the chair. They handcuffed the leg of the chair to the table and left the room, looking back with satisfaction. The sound of the door locking in place made Ivy shake –she hated feeling vulnerable.

CHAPTER 19

Adam and Finch met again at Jack's house.

"We stopped by Ivy's place, she's gone. We think the men who attacked Finch, kidnapped her, too," Adam said.

"Did you search her apartment?" he asked.

"There was nothing there. They must have taken her soon after we dropped her off. She put up a good fight, the place was wrecked," Finch said. "But, one of them dropped a cell phone at my place. Check it out."

"Let's put in a call and give Agent Powell what she wants. Let's end this," Jack said.

"I can't believe this is my life. When did we become the superpowers?" Adam asked.

"I think that's the point – that anybody can be powerful, given the right motivation," Finch said.

Jack thought about what Finch said and it was finally making sense. He had questioned his purpose in a way and wondered how he had ended up here —wherever here was. Could it really have been as simple as motivation? We do what we are motivated to do – is that it? He almost felt ashamed. Maybe the advice people gave him – to find himself – was a way of saying that *you* make choices. Looking back, Jack recognized that after his mother died, his dad made a choice – a choice to get up every morning and make a life —whatever that meant — for his family and *that* was his motivation: family.

Adam snapped his fingers in Jack's face to get his attention, "Are you with us – don't get all weird on us now, okay? So, where does that take us – what now?"

"Simple, Jack said. "We follow the yellow brick road." Adam and Finch looked in Jack's direction, placing their palms face up as if to ask "what?" Jack continued. "Well, Finch, if you can hack into a few computers, we can gather the phone numbers this guy dialed, get the addresses and see where they lead. Before we do that – I'll call in a missing person report to the police. That way, they can work from their end and we can work on our leads – we don't want to take any unnecessary chances."

Finch took out his bag of tools and sat down at the computer. He took the cables and plugged the cell phone into the computer and began to feel his way around the keypad, which was specially-designed with Braille keys – which enabled him to easily type as capably and efficiently as anyone else. "Adam, if you'll let me know once we've entered the directory, I'll try a few codes and see if that will get us into the network," Finch said.

Adam watched as Finch expertly managed to tap into the network and reveal the phone numbers dialed in the past month.

"Amazing, that was fantastic!"

"That's why I get paid the big bucks!" Finch said. "Actually, they don't change the codes all that often and I have a program that randomly converts numbers and codes until it locks on to one very specific sequence that fits."

"I take it you wrote that program," Adam said smiling – already knowing the answer.

"Yes, it is my program – I guess that means not only do I get the big bucks, but I'm worth it." Finch said. "It's nothing any other handsomely charming, Greek Adonis–like genius couldn't have done."

"Can we get address for these numbers?" Jack interrupted their conversation.

"If they're land lines, it will be easier, but we can track the numbers to the accounts and see what we find," Adam said.

"Guys we are making this way too complicated – let's just call the last number dialed and see who answers," Jack said, making the phone call. "Hello – who is this? I'm sorry; I have the wrong number, thank you."

Jack turned to Finch and Adam. "It was just a pizza delivery restaurant – it was worth a shot."

"Maybe more than that," Adam said. "These guys must realize their phone is missing – what if that was just a ruse?"

"So you think they knew it was us and they were trying to throw us off?" Finch asked.

"That would be my bet," Adam said. "Look – see, this number matches the one we called – and it's not in an area zoned for businesses. I know the area – there are warehouses near the docks. Let's go see what we find there."

Jack grabbed the keys to the Dartz Prombron and they gathered some supplies and headed to the car.

"When we get there, let's keep a low profile – we don't want to be noticed. Let's keep our distance and observe okay. And watch each other backs," Jack said.

"*We're* supposed to keep a low profile in this thing? Do you own a car that isn't unnecessarily flashy and over the top? They're gonna see us coming in this thing!" Adam said.

Finch walked alongside the SUV feeling the surface of the car as he walked. He was a connoisseur of cars and knew everything about them. He could just about identify any car by touch; he had a sixth sense when it came to cars. Finch paused as he bent down to slide his hand along the rims, careful not to miss any details. He stood upright and snapped his head around to face Jack, "No way! This is the Dartz Prombrom Red Diamond edition, right? I'm right aren't I?" He continued to assess the car and underneath the hood.

"It's so major. This is off the charts amazing. It's got gold–plated bulletproof windows and bulletproof wheels... This is a sweet car. I could live in this car, seriously" Finch exclaimed. "I'm marrying your car."

"I think he is in love with my car," Jack told Adam.

They all loaded into the truck and drove to the warehouse.

"Tell me if you see anything interesting ok?" Finch said. "I'll just relax and enjoy the seat, which is softer than my bed at home."

"We won't leave you out, don't worry," Adam said, looking through the binoculars and ducking down. "No one can see us through these windows, right?"

"I hope Ivy's okay – it's got to be killing her to be locked up somewhere," Finch said. "If I know her, she's trying to figure out her own rescue plan and it likely involves kicking the butts of men twice her size – that's what worries me. We've got to get them before anything really bad happens."

"They need them alive. Ivy and Sarah should be safe," Jack said. "At least for now – it's just a matter of giving them what they want (or at least making them think we are giving them what they want). I guess that means you're starting to care about Ivy? He looked at Finch and felt a twinge of jealousy – which he would never admit aloud. It wasn't a guy thing and well, he wasn't about to give Adam ammunition to use against him – they would never let him get over it if he admitted that he wanted to be as open about his feelings for Sarah. So, he did what guys do; he dropped the subject and started talking about cars.

CHAPTER 20

"Look, those guys are going into the warehouse – they look familiar, don't they Jack? Where have I seen them?" Adam asked.

They are the same men that we saw on the video from the coffee shop – they kidnapped my dad. Let's think about this for a minute. Jack stared silently toward the warehouse for a moment.

"Let's get closer and see if we can find out what's going on inside," Adam suggested. If we tail them, sooner or later, they've got to lead us back to Agent Powell. She hasn't exactly been out in the open these days."

"Maybe," Jack thought aloud – but eventually *she* will contact *us*. I mean, we have something she wants, so she has to talk to us. The only reason she has waited is because she was trying to stack things in her favor and make it impossible for me to say no to her request. Now that she has Sarah and Ivy, it won't be too long. "Wait," Jack said, – leaning forward in his seat. He watched the same two men exit the warehouse and pause outside the door. "What are they doing?"

Adam suddenly ducked down, using his hand to shield his face. "I think they're looking at us."

Jack started the engine and said, "No. They don't seem to be looking at us. But, maybe we should move further back just in case." Jack put the truck in reverse and started to back away onto the dirt road. As soon as he did so, things started to blur.

Adam said "They're headed this way." Several men ran out of the building with guns and started shooting. Jack started the car and started to drive away. The van followed closely and pulled in the lane beside them, rolled down the window and shot at the car at close range. Adam and Jack ducked – and sighed relief when the bullets bounced off the window.

Finch said, "This truck is coming in handy after all."

Jack drove expertly, racing at top speeds down the road. Looking into his rear view mirror, he saw that the car was about to overtake them. Jack grabbed the steering wheel tightly and guided the tuck into the lane just in front of the car blocking their path.

"Hold on guys," Jack said. Then, in a move that would have been suicidal with most vehicles, Jack stomped hard on the brakes, coming to a complete stop, allowing the car behind him to ram into them from behind. The small car spiraled off the road and flipped over.

"That was fun guys – not quite the walk in the park that I was hoping for," Finch said,

Jack turned the truck around and headed back toward the flipped over car.

"What are you doing," Adam asked. "Are you crazy – those guys have guns?"

"I know what I'm doing," Jack told the guys. "You can stay in the truck if you'd like, but I'm going to get some answers. They were shooting at us for a reason – so they must know who we are. Let's find out what they know.

"Just be careful," Adam said.

Jack pulled near the car that was turned on its side and approached slowly. He walked to the side of the car, bent down to look inside and turned back toward his truck. Adam and Finch got out of the truck and walked toward Jack, "What's going on," Adam asked.

"Nothing" Jack said. "They're gone – no one is in the car. That's probably the fastest getaway in history. Let's go."

"A second car was probably following them and picked them up," Finch said. "There is no way they could have gotten away that quickly otherwise."

"The next phone number on the list is just five miles away, we can stop by," Adam said. "Hopefully no one will be shooting at us this time – and I'm staying in the car, just in case anybody's wondering."

Jack drove to the university and parked in the lot facing the building. He shut off the engine and looked around.

"Are you sure the number was from this location?"

"Of course, I'm sure. But what would those men have been looking for here," Adam asked.

Jack sighed. "I don't know. They went inside and Jack walked toward Sarah's classroom. They weaved in and out of the crowded hallway, speaking to classmates as they passed. "Hey Jack, I heard about the party. Jack turned to face a blonde girl, dressed in designer jeans and a backless halter top.

"What party," Jack asked innocently.

"Adam told me all about it," she said, looking at Adam. Two other girls grabbed her and pulled her into their conversation and she walked away. She turned and yelled, "I can't wait!"

Jack stared down the hall and then turned to Adam. "What was that about – what party?"

"You remember. You agreed to have a party after finals at your house. I just kind of forgot to cancel – what with all the gunfire, missing people and helicopter trips to Texas– but I will. Don't worry about it," Adam laughed.

"Am I invited," Finch asked.

"Of course – I mean if there *were* a party," Adam said, then looked at Jack, "which there isn't."

Jack stopped in front of Sarah's office and turned the handle.

"Great, the door is locked." He looked around. "Maybe I could break the door without causing too much attention."

Finch stepped forward in front of Jack.

"Step aside. Give me one minute and this can be taken care of neatly and quietly."

Finch took a small black pouch from his back pocket and opened it to reveal various silver tools.

"Cover me – tell me if anyone comes this way," he said.

Finch started to work on the door lock.

"It's just a little something that I learned growing up on the streets. Everything isn't fancy cars, mansions and yachts."

"What streets? You didn't…," Adam started to say.

"Fine – I didn't," Finch interrupted. "I learned it on the internet – I ordered an instructional learning program, *okay! Are you happy? Do you have to ruin everything?* It's part of my persona – it's a more interesting story than books, thesis papers and research. Finch stood up and exhaled, "Voila` – we're in."

"All my friends are weird. I might possibly be the last sane person on the planet. I'm completely serious. You are both mental – you realize that, don't you," Adam asked.

Jack moved past Finch and Adam – completely ignoring Adam's comments. Jack looked at the door lock and patted Finch on the back. "Excellent. That was very nicely done." He held the door open as Adam and Finch entered. Jack looked up and down the hallway and then closed the door behind them. Finch stayed near the door. He was the obvious choice for the lookout. He could easily hear someone approaching in time to warn Adam and Jack.

They moved around the office quietly, searching the shelves and desk for anything that seemed odd or out of place.

"What do you think they wanted in here," Adam asked. He picked up a stack of papers and flipped quickly through them.

Jack spoke in a hushed tone, "They were definitely in here," he said grimly. Jack picked up a book from the shelf and replaced it back in its original place. He moved over to the desk. It was an antique vintage pedestal desk with burl inlays – it fit well. This was definitely her space. She had filled it with personal items unique only to her.

"They were watching her – just like they've probably been watching all of us," Jack said. Sarah is kind of OCD about order. I was in her office before and she had a distinct order in how she placed things – I'm not even sure if she's aware that she does it. Books are always on the shelves alphabetically by the author's name. I saw that at her house as well. These papers should have been in date order – someone was looking for something. They tried to put things back in their proper places, but they didn't know about the OCD – it's not something that would have been apparent to someone, initially."

Jack ran his hands alongside the desk and the drawers. The wood around the front drawer had visible signs of forced entry. The wood looked as if it had been chipped away. Jack picked up pieces of wood from the floor underneath the desk.

Adam saw Jack bent underneath the desk. "What is it?" Did you find something?"

"Not really," he said, "but someone tried to get in the desk drawer; I don't think they did. Maybe someone surprised them; I don't know. Or maybe, they just weren't as good with locks as Finch," Jack said smiling.

Jack searched the computer files and the history on Sarah's computer. Even now, he liked being near her things. It made him feel like she was close by. He would make it a point to find out more about her family and what she liked to do in her leisure and where, if there was one place that she could visit in the world, where that might be. Jack had to shake his head to stop the endless path of questions that he wanted answered about Sarah.

"Someone downloaded a copy of her files."

Adam placed a journal in front of Jack. "Look – pages have been torn from her calendar."

Jack took the journal and inspected the book closer. He took the book and opened it – shaking it. A single picture fell from between the pages. He knew the face immediately from pictures from inside her home.

"A picture of her father," Jack said, as he replaced it and placed the book gently back on the desk. "Well, someone knew her comings and goings – it wouldn't have taken much to determine where she would be and follow her. They could have taken her anytime.

Finch still leaned against the door with his ear pressed against it. "Hurry up – classes will be switching any minute now."

"Let's go," Jack said. "Before leaving the office, Jack turned off the lights and the room darkened, except for a noticeable glow in the corner. On the bottom shelf was the project that he had made for a class assignment– the battery-powered cell. The corners of Jack's mouth hinted a smile. It was the first day they had met – a day he would never forget. He locked the door and closed it tightly.

As soon as the three closed the door to Sarah's office, doors opened from all over the hall. Students crammed noisily into the hallways. A group of very large boys wearing shorts and flip flops approached Jack and his friends, holding up flyers.

"We heard about the party – thanks for the invite," one of the boys said, looking at Jack with excitement. They walked around Jack and joined another group of girls.

Jack looked immediately at Adam, rolling his eyes. "I know. I know," Adam said. "Stop worrying. It's taken care of – not a problem. We've got more important things to think about anyway. Don't you agree?" Jack shook his head in frustration.

"Break it up, guys – let's get out of here," Finch said.

Adam stiffened and moved slowly trying to blend into the crowd.

"Jack, there are two men in black suits coming this way – I don't think they're students, do you?"

Jack looked down the hall and quickly looked away. "Maybe they didn't see us. Let's go the other way."

Jack, Finch and Adam walked with another group of students through the hallway, making conversation and trying to look inconspicuous. Jack looked around to find that the men were still following.

"New plan – run!" Jack ran and Finch and Adam followed close behind. "The music room – head to the music room – I have an idea," Jack said.

Jack ran as fast as he could to the music room. He knew it would be empty this time of day and they would be out of the way of innocent people passing by. Finch and Adam took the corridor to the right – a longer route but the easiest to maneuver for Finch. Jack reached the music room first and hid behind the stage curtains. Finch and Adam arrived shortly after, with the men in black close behind.

Jack motioned for Adam to run across the stage from the west side. Adam immediately knew what Jack planned. The men lunged forward missing both Adam and Finch. Once they had passed a certain place on stage Jack yelled, "NOW!" Adam and Finch leapt across the orchestra pit and Jack waved his hands to the side, opening a door to the floor pit. The men fell inside. Jack quickly closed the door shut – trapping them.

"As soon as you mentioned the music room, I knew where you were going – it was good thinking. It worked pretty nicely, too. Let's leave before they send someone else after us. I have had enough chasing for one day," Adam grumbled.

Jack arrived at the coffee shop.

"Wow, this is where my dad was taken – look!" Jack said. Three men in black suits came out of the coffee shop and got into a van. Jack followed them to a dead-end street and then the van was gone. Jack's phone rang and he quickly answered it.

Agent Powell was on the line, "Hello Jack."

Jack seethed, "I want my friends back, now."

Agent Powell scoffed and responded more casually, "Civility is lost on today's youth -- no one has manners anymore."

"Did you hear me? Where are Sarah and Ivy?" Jack yelled.

"Anything to stop you from chasing my men all around town – we're not going to get anywhere that way," Agent Powell responded. "Come to the warehouse on Greenbay Park Road near the waterfront in thirty minutes. Bring the battery chip, I know you have it."

"I'll be there, but if you don't release my friends, I'm going to break you into pieces," Jack said, as he hung up the phone.

Jack made a u–turn – we have to make a stop. And you need to pick up your car."

"Why– what's going on," Adam wanted to know.

Jack hit the steering wheel and came to a complete stop, pounding his fist against the wheel. He turned to Adam and Finch – "That was Agent Powell. She wants me to meet her on Greenbay with the chip. I've got to go home – there are some things we're going to need."

"Jack… is there a chip," Adam asked.

Jack just kept driving until he got home. Finch and Adam followed him inside. They gathered rope, guns, two-way radios and Finch took his lock-picking tools. .

Jack summoned Haley, "Come here Haley – I'm sorry to have to do this, but you have something we need. Don't worry – we'll return it. Haley sat at Jack's feet – Good girl," he said. Jack opened the compartment near Haley's head and removed a flat, gold, chip. Everyone watched as the light went out of Haley's eyes until she no longer moved. Everyone was staring at Jack. They knew Haley was a robot – and technically, she was not real, but was something very saddening watching it – it was strange. Jack broke the weirdness of the moment and said, "Let's go."

"Whoa," Adam said. "Do we need to have a moment of silence...?"

Jack ignored Adam and pushed past them saying, "I'll take my car, you guys follow in Adam's car...but not too close. Listen on your earpieces for Agent Powell to tell the location. I will hand over the battery only after I talk to the girls on the phone. That will force her to have to call their location and that's when you do a satellite trace. Leave immediately when you get the location. Leave me to take care of Agent Powell."

"I'm not sure that's the best plan, Jack. We don't want to split up – the best defense is going to be in our numbers – wouldn't you say," Finch asked. "What if something goes unexpectedly wrong – you could use another set of eyes."

"I don't trust this anymore that you two. But we can't take any chances – the most important thing is to get Ivy and Sarah to safety. I will be fine," Jack insisted.

Adam shook his head as if doubting Jack. He didn't like any of this – he would rather they found a way to keep everyone together. Separating was always a bad thing – didn't they watch the movies?

CHAPTER 21

Jack drove to Greenbay Road and parked close to the building. He spoke into his earpiece to Adam and Finch to stick to the plan and listen for Sarah and Ivy's location.

"Listen guys, for this to work, you have to do this – you leave immediately when she gives the location – don't wait for me. I'll be close behind."

"So, you're part of Sector 12," Jack asked. "Did my father know?"

Laughing, Agent Powell responded, "I *am* Sector 12. I started the organization. Your father was a naive fool. He didn't know anything. He didn't know I was stealing his designs. We first started trading secrets and then weapons. Your father was very instrumental."

"My father was not a fool. He trusted you," Jack said.

"Yes, and he was wrong to do so, wasn't he?" Agent Powell smiled menacingly, he should have known – or maybe he did, but he dismissed it. That too, was weak. Did you bring the battery," Agent Powell asked.

Jack stared at her, determined to get the information he needed first. Finch and Adam were counting on him. "I need to talk to the girls first."

Agent Powell glared into Jack's eyes, studying his face, trying to read his demeanor. Jack looked back with added resolve – he did not give an inch as he waited for Agent Powell to respond. She turned to one of her men and nodded to another. He picked up a cell phone and made a call, handing the phone to Jack.

"Hello," Jack spoke loudly, with an urgency that could easily be interpreted as desperation. He caught himself and stood taller, steadying his voice, so that he spoke more evenly. "Hello," Jack said again, "Is anybody there?"

"Jack, this is Sarah," her voice sounded strained. "I'm here with Ivy,   we   were   kidnapped."
"I know – I'm going to help you. Did they hurt you?" Jack asked.

"We're fine – we're on a ….." Sarah tried to finish by letting them know they were on a boat before the phone was taken from her. The guard was much too quick, jerking the phone away from her, almost pushing her over in the progress. "We will be fine," Sarah whispered to herself. "We'll be fine," she repeated over and over again. The more Sarah repeated the words, the more certain she became that it was true."

"Your friends are fine for now, but their danger increases with every minute that passes. Give me the Power chip, now," Agent Powell said.

"Fine," Jack said. He reached hesitantly into his jacket and pulled out a slim metal box. Jack held his hands high in the air, before handing the box over to her. "You did not deserve my father's trust," he said.

"Your father was unreasoned, foolish and ill–advised. He was weak. He wanted peace among the nations," Agent Powell said.

"*And that made him unreasoned and foolish – because he wanted peace?*" Jack asked with a sarcastic tone.

"No, because he believed it was actually possible and sacrificed himself to achieve it," Powell shouted. "You could do so much more, if you choose. We are similar, you and I – much more than Frank – more than he ever conceived possible," she said.

"I'm my father's son – sorry," Jack said.

The men took the chip over to Agent Powell, who immediately inserted it into a device, which lit up and displayed images across her screen. "Perfect, Agent Powell said. "It is a thing of beauty."

Agent Powell looked upon the battery as if it were the Holy Grail – she hovered over it, passionately – rarely looking away, as if in a trance.

"Where are my friends? You said you would tell me where they are. I have held up my end of the bargain," Jack stated.

"Fine – I will tell you," she said. "But it won't do you any good. "They're on a boat twenty-five miles from the bay," Agent Powell said casually, as if she were reciting a phone number. "But, unfortunately for them, in ten minutes, the ship is going to blow up. You're going to be a little busy, I'm afraid."

Agent Powell glanced at her guards. "Kill him," she demanded. "Make sure he doesn't leave the building. She then turned to remove the battery and place it in her pouch. But during those few seconds that Agent Powell had looked away, Jack had held out his hands and battery was in his possession at speed of light. Jack had seen the transaction, but the movement was much too fast for anyone else's eyes. Agent Powell made her way toward the stairs – she exited the stairwell door to board the waiting helicopter on the roof. "…and now, I've got the power," she yelled back as the door slammed behind her.

This was her escape route. If she thought that she was going to get off that easy, she was mistaken, Jack thought to himself.

Jack had too much on the line to let her walk out, leaving so much damage behind. He would not let her get away with Frank's death. It was not revenge, so much as principal. And of course, there was the promise.

Jack dived behind some metal shelves as bullets started to fly from every direction. Jack thought aloud, "Every action has an equal and opposite reaction."

From across the room, Jack peered behind the shelves. He saw a crowbar on the floor and reacted violently – using his mind to lift it off the ground and send it spiraling toward one of the gunmen. The crowbar hit the gunman's rifle and flipped it wildly into the air. The rifle hit another gunman's rifle, sending that man's rifle spiraling, and his rifle, forced a third gunman's rifle into the air – until there was a ripple effect that ended with every rifle in the room piled on the floor in broken pieces. Jack was sure there had never been anything like it. The guards, wounded and dazed – never saw what hit them.

Jack looked around for the ramp that led to the stairs. He knew time was running out for Ivy and Sarah. He could only hope that Finch and Adam would get there in time enough to save them before the ship blew up. Jack ran up the stairs to the roof, the wind from the helicopter almost knocking him over. Agent Powell was already safely inside and buckling up for takeoff. She stared at Jack with satisfaction, almost smiling, with the look of someone who had just won the game and taken the prize. Jack had to think quickly.

Police sirens were approaching. All of this would be over soon, Jack thought to himself. The most important thing was to get the girls home safe. Jack thought again to his friends – he used those thoughts to inspire him…to energize him to get out quickly.

"Force equals mass times acceleration," Jack yelled over the noise of the propellers, and then picked up a brick and sent it hurling into the helicopter's propeller. When the brick made contact, it sent out an electrical spark – a current that flashed blue lights into the night. The helicopter slowed and rocked wildly back and forth before starting to nose dive. From inside the helicopter, Jack could see Agent Powell's face stiffen. Her mouth gaped open as the realization of her imminent doom became apparent.

Jack exhaled from relief and sheer exhaustion.

"Knowledge really is power – what do you know," Jack said to himself, as he stood on the edge of the roof. His eyes winced tightly when the helicopter crashed into the ground. The metal smashed and folded in half. It was twisted and crumpled – barely recognizable. There were broken pieces of metal covering the ground – thrown in every direction for miles. The pilot was thrown from the helicopter as it plummeted. Agent Powell's body still lay inside – her body slumped forward. Her arm mangled in the broken glass. Jack looked at his watch and turned away from the smoking wreckage and found the nearest exit.

He nearly ran – glad to be away from the crumpled mess. He wanted to be gone from this. He wanted to get back to a place of normalcy. But first, he had to get to his friends. Jack hopped in his car, slamming the door shut and shifting the gears urgently. He pushed the car as fast as it would go.

"I have to get there in time – I just have to," he said to himself.

THE POWER

CHAPTER 22

Jack made it to the docks in record speed. His body started to tremble as he leapt out of the car and ran toward the boats. Jack's face was completely blank – he did not allow himself to think – he just ran.

He made it to the edge of the shore just in time to see smoke-filled clouds in the distance offshore. He slowed and was knocked off–balance as the noise registered in his brain. And then, there was another explosion, followed by thick black smoke hovering in the air.

"No!" Jack yelled as he jumped onto one of the boats, still determined to get closer. Pieces of ash floated in the air as his mind began to sink in despair, knowing that he had put his friends in danger and now caused their deaths.

Jack looked up – there was another noise in the distance. He could hear the roaring from an engine approaching. He started to smile, as he tried to focus his eyes – he could hear the engine getting stronger as it neared the shore. Jack's heart started to pound loudly against his chest – he didn't even realize how hard he was breathing. Jack waved his hands back and forth wildly, smiling uncontrollably – he could just make out his friends' faces as they came closer. He sighed in relief seeing that Adam, Finch, Sarah and Ivy were on board.

Ivy and Sarah jumped off the boat first – they were soaked and their clothes disheveled, but they were clearly unharmed, running under their own power. Adam and Finch ran behind them. Everyone collapsed around Jack and hugged each other.

"Other than bumps and bruises, the girls are fine," Adam spoke first. "When we arrived, most of the guards had already gone. Apparently, two stayed to make sure the explosion went off and they had an escape float near the boat for a quick and easy get–away."

Adam looked at Jack, and then back at Finch.

"You should have seen me, Jack. Those guards didn't know what hit them. I used the jujitsu technique that Ivy had shown us earlier and I got the jump on him. I flipped him overboard and it was easy for us then to find the room where they were keeping Sarah and Ivy. We transported the girls back to our boat just as the boat started to blow.

Sarah hugged Jack tightly between laughter. Jack looked bewildered at the group. He couldn't process the strange atmosphere – but ignored it…just happy they were safe and Sarah was in his arms.

Ivy caught Jack up to date on what happened from the moment that Finch and Adam arrived, but Finch had a different version.

Finch laughed hysterically. "Jack – Adam didn't tell the complete story. That's not how I remember it all," he said. "When we got to the boat, the deck was empty, we climbed on board and then two guards rushed toward us. I did the Indian Death move that Ivy showed us and flipped the guy overboard. Then the second guard grabbed me from behind. I karate kicked him into a door and that's where we found Sarah and Ivy tied up. Adam and I untied them and got back on our boat just as we heard the explosion. The force of the explosion almost turned our boat over – we barely got away. We drove away through fire and smoke – it was crazy. That's when Adam saw you standing on the shore. It was a wild ride," Finch said, finally taking a breath.

"Well, I may never really know what happened out there but thanks guys. I'm sorry I put you in the middle of this," Jack said.

"Are you kidding, it was the best time I've ever had," Adam said.

"I've definitely had better," Sarah said.

"That's it, Adam asked? It's over? What's next?"

"We live to fight another day guys. Go home and get some sleep," Jack said.

Jack drove Sarah home in silence. At the door, Sarah quickly said goodnight.

"Wait, that's all?" Jack asked. "You could stay with me," Jack began.

Sarah turned slowly toward him. "Look Jack, thank you so much for risking your life to save mine. I'm very grateful – truly I am. But I had a lot of time to think while I was tied up," Sarah spoke slowly. "I care about you. You were all I thought about. I knew you would come for me. I never once doubted that you would come. The thought kept me from losing my mind. But, you're not the *relationship* type of guy. You don't know what you're going to do from one day to the next. You've suffered loss and are still trying to work through that – I get that you're trying to figure out who you are, but I know who *I* am already." Sarah took Jack's hand. "Try not to take this the wrong way. You may be the smartest guy I've ever known, but you have a lot to learn."

Jack looked at Sarah, wanting to stop her from going in the house. He had a hundred questions. He wanted to say so much, but the words would not come. There was nothing to say. They just stood there for a while, as if the night would bring answers.

"Goodnight Jack," Sarah final said. She stood on her tip toes and kissed him goodnight before going inside, leaving Jack on her doorstep, confused.

Jack went home and sank down into his chair. He removed the battery chip from his pocket and placed it back inside Haley. The room lit up as an image of Jack's father emanated from Haley and hovered above her.

"Jack, if you're listening to this message, I'm probably dead," Frank's image said. "I just wanted you to know that your mother and I always believed in you. You are destined to do great things. All my research, my life's work is about you...not a chip, not formulas, but faith in powers we saw in you, even when you were little. We have always known that you would find your way. Never underestimate the power inside you. When you feel most alone, know that I am near...I will always be around, Jack."

Jack sat in silence for a long time. Then, as if drawn by deep need, Jack picked up his guitar and played quietly in the night. This was familiarity. There were no lyrics – he just allowed the music to take him away. Jack thought about his past...his parents, who he would never see again. For the first time, he felt connected in a way that fueled him and gave him renewed inspiration. He knew now, that his parents would live forever inside him. The more he continued in their teachings and their work – they would never really be gone.

Jack thought of his friends and how they were there to help when he most needed them. He never thought of himself as lucky before now. Jack was seeing more clearly now. He could not have hand-picked three more loyal and trustworthy friends, if he tried – there had to be something to that. The thought made him hopeful.

It wasn't long before the images in Jack's head turned to Sarah. She had her own distinctive place in his heart. She was already so much a part of him – she filled his mind, she became the inspiration in his music...she was in every breath. Jack laughed aloud so hard that he could barely stop. He was beginning to think and believe that for the first time, his future could be something slightly resembling wonderful. Wonderful had not been a part of his vocabulary before he met Sarah but the world was a vastly different place with her in it.

That night Jack dreamed as he slept. There were no bad memories, or painful images. Tonight there was only tranquility and rest.

CHAPTER 23

Sarah woke surprisingly refreshed – like she had been on an extended vacation instead of being held captive on a boat. She breathed in, filling her lungs until no more air could enter, and then exhaled, slowly. The morning brought with it a strange, but inviting unfamiliarity. Everything was the same and yet everything was different. The experiences of the prior weeks had completely redefined her. As she stared at her reflection in the bathroom mirror, the face looking back at her seemed almost unrecognizable. Sarah fixated on the image…something was off. Was it the eyes? Or maybe the smile, she wondered. Sarah didn't know what to make of the transformation. She looked at her watch and hurried off to the university.

Sarah had started extra early to prepare because today was final exams. The day would be a long one. She would have to administer the test for all of her classes. The Dean had been very cooperative and agreed to let Sarah continue her classes. Sarah had an excellent reputation with the university and her credentials impeccable. They easily let her jump right back in where she left off, with the promise to try to get word to them the next time she had a *family emergency*. After the completion of Sarah's first two class sessions, she noticed that the classes and students were the same, but still, there was something very distinctly different about the way she saw the world.

Sarah stood at the front of the class, as students entered to take the Physics exam.

"Good morning, Professor London, good to have you back," one of the students told her, taking an exam booklet, then sitting near the back. Sarah continued to hand out exam books, not really stopping to look at faces.

"Good morning," another student said. In return, Sarah merely said, "good morning," looking away, blankly.

Sarah wrote the exam instructions on the board, but was startled when a friendly voice spoke, "Hello Sarah — I mean, Professor London." It was Adam, smiling big and wide, as if he were hiding a secret that Sarah would want to know. He took an exam book and took a seat up front. Adam motioned to the door, nodding his head. Sarah glanced around to see Jack walking toward her.

For a moment, Sarah thought she might have been dreaming. But the closer he got, her senses confirmed that he was real. She hated that she got all giddy when he was around. He had a way of making her feel like she was back in grade school, when love felt like it was life or death, bringing about emotions so strong that you swore you couldn't breathe without him – the object of your love. It was fierce and dramatic – that's the way she felt seeing Jack now.

"Professor," Jack said simply.

Sarah extended her hand and gave Jack an exam book. During the exchange, their hands touched briefly. It was soft and gentle and it was over much too quickly, Sarah's thought. Jack smiled at Sarah and took the vacant seat next to Adam. She braced herself and completed the instructions. She suddenly felt light-headed and nervous as she announced, "You will have exactly two hours to complete the exam. You may turn in your booklet when you are finished and leave."

Sarah looked at the clock and said slowly, "The exam...starts...now. Good luck everyone."

Sarah watched Jack, as he took the test – moving expertly through the questions at superhuman speed. He looked very competent, sitting there. Every now and again, Jack would glance up at her, causing Sarah to lose her breath. She had to look away to regain composure.

Jack was the first to complete the exam. He quietly walked to the front of the room and handed in his booklet and left without a word. He left without even a backward glance. Sarah stared mindlessly at the door after he had gone.

"Oh, I hate him," she said under her breath. A second after the words left her lips, she immediately laughed at herself. She looked around the room at the students still taking tests. She hoped none of them had seen her talking to herself – it wasn't the most professional and mature way to behave she was sure – but she couldn't help it.

I love him, she thought. I've lost my mind...and I love him.

One by one, students completed their exams. The last student finally left, closing the door behind him. Sarah exhaled and sat there alone. Her day was not over yet – she thought. She grabbed the exam books to take home to grade. She was filled with anticipation and looking forward to her next adventure.

*

Adam tapped his foot impatiently as he waited for Jack to answer the door.

Jack opened the door and Adam yelled, "Finals are over– it's party time!"

Jack's eyes widened, "What are you talking about, Adam?"

Adam repeated the phrase slowly with exaggeration, "It's... party... time. As in, 'it's...time... to... get... our... party... on!'"

It's a colloquial, dude. Try to keep up." Adam danced around waving his arms from side to side. He sang repeatedly, "It's time to party. It's time to party!"

Jack squinted his eyes, causing his forehead to wrinkle. He looked sternly at Adam then spoke, "Tell me you canceled the party!"

"Why would I do that?" Adam shouted.

"Because you told me that you would," Jack yelled. "There is *not* going to be a party here tonight. No way!"

"The party is already underway – take a look," Adam said.

Jack stood for a second, taking in Adam's words. He slowly walked outside as cars filled his driveway and people leapt out in groups and headed to the backyard. Jack followed the crowd around back – which led to an even larger crowd of party-goers in shorts and swimsuits jumping into the pool.

Adam slapped Jack on the back and said, "You can thank me later."

"Thank you?" Jack asked sarcastically.

He was at a loss for words. He looked around. It seemed like the whole school was in his backyard.

"At least they're having fun. But, I don't think they'd notice if I was here or not – or would care," Jack he said.

"Well, I wouldn't quite say that," Adam laughed. "There are a couple of people that I know for sure would care whether you're here or not. Take a look toward the pool house."

Jack looked into the crowd and quickly spotted Finch and Ivy. They made their way over to Jack.

"We wouldn't have missed your party for the world. Thanks for the invite," Ivy said.

"Anytime," Jack said as he looked suspiciously at Adam.

"I would like to be kept informed the next time there is a party thrown at my house, Adam. But you all are always invited. I'm glad you're here. Enjoy the party!" Jack watched as Ivy and Finch danced away. Ivy danced mostly and dragged Finch along for the ride.

All of a sudden, Jack was really glad Adam didn't cancel the party. He could get used to this – friends. It felt nice.

"Things are about to get even better," Adam said, moving aside and point toward the house.

Jack looked up and saw Sarah standing in his doorway.

"Sarah," Jack whispered.

Adam patted him on the back. "I think you can handle it from here."

Adam left Jack and joined some friends in the crowd. He climbed the ladder and walked onto the diving board, then stood on the very edge and yelled, "Cannonball!"

Jack was focused on one person. He walked toward Sarah, reaching for her, "You're here." Jack picked Sarah up and spun her around. He placed her gently on the ground, letting his arm fall gently on the small of her back.

"I'm here," Sarah breathed. There was no place on earth she would have rather have been. She jumped at the chance to come when Adam called. She had only graded a handful of tests when the phone rang. She dropped everything eagerly for the chance to see Jack again.

"Why aren't you outside with the others," Jack asked, taking her hand and leading her deeper inside the house.

"Well, I don't think they need a chaperone and having a teacher at the party may seem awkward. Sarah never took her eyes away from Jack as she spoke.

"I thought you should know you got an A. You answered every question correctly, although I'm not surprised."

Jack smiled, "I told you – I do very well on exams."

"I didn't know you very well then," Sarah said. "I thought you were overconfident, bragging and trying too hard to impress me at the time…hmm, you were just telling the truth it seems."

Jack used his power to pull Sarah closer. He snapped his fingers and her wrap gently fell to the floor, revealing her bathing suit underneath. Jack leaned down and sent a trail of kisses up Sarah's neck.

"Someone told me once that I have a lot to learn," Jack said between kisses.

Sarah reached up and curled her arm around Jack's neck. She pressed into him and put her head against his chest. "Well, let me be the first to say that you show great promise."

ABOUT THE AUTHOR

Sherian McCoy is an author and conference speaker. The central theme in all of her messages is "you've got more power than you know."

She has earned a Bachelor's degree from Texas Woman's University, a Master's degree from Southern Methodist University and a Juris Doctorate from Texas Wesleyan School of Law.

Sherian and her husband, Ike, are the proud parents of two daughters, Ivy Grace and Sarah Elizabeth.

WWW.MARTINSISTERSPUBLISHING.COM